TURNED BY THE PAWN

MURDOCH MAFIA SERIES
BOOK 5

SAMANTHA BARRETT

Robbie,
My man of honor, my kids godfather, this one's for you, my
cousin.
I love you and appreciate you more than you will ever know!
Keep it real...

This book may make some uncomfortable with the content.

I have always sworn if I ever wrote a Mafia book I would go dark,
in order to stay true to my characters. That is what I have done.
Some scenes and descriptions may make you uneasy,
make you feel squeamish but rest assured, there is an HEA.
For those who have read my PNR and thought they were
dark, well this is worse, so much worse but in the best way
possible.

Welcome to the Murdoch Mafia and all their fucked up
shit.

Prologue

Gage

Six weeks...

I manage to keep my word and get into the Bratva as a foot solider. I'm stuck guarding the outside of the club they operate in, never getting a glimpse inside. I haven't even laid eyes on the Pakhan himself only a couple of his captains, one of them being the fucker that shot my brother. The morgue's result came back no match. Bishop and King have given up hope that Rook is alive but Knight hasn't, and neither have I. To give up hope means to give up on Rook and that is something I can't do. I will never give up on my family. Bishop and I may not see eye to eye all the time but he is blood. I would die for my brothers and sister in a heartbeat. The crackle of my radio pulls me from my thoughts. I wait with bated breath hoping by some fucking miracle that I manage to get some information or a chance to see Vlad.

"We got a situation out back, go clean it." I grind my teeth to keep from telling the Russian fucker to suck my dick. Their English is so fucking bad you can barely understand the fuckers. I've been studying Russian and learning to speak it since I first found out about them going against my family. I need to be able to understand what they are saying if we are going to end this. We've managed to pinpoint who most of the politicians are that work for Vlad thanks to Knight and Vin hacking their bank records and finding large sums deposited into their accounts. "Hurry up!"

"I'm nearly there," I growl. I'm so fucking over this shit. I'm not the type of guy who can sit behind a desk like Bishop or play on a laptop all day like Knight. Fuck if I know what King does. Vin and I are the same, we're hands on guys and like to settle things that way. I slam to a stop when I reach the back of the club, the bass from the music is louder around this side. I look around the poorly lit alley that holds the dumpsters but see nothing. I'm about to radio back when a figure shifts out of the shadows. I draw my gun and aim at the person's head, waiting for them to make a move into the light so I can see their face.

"I'm not here to fight."

"You're American?" And a girl, but I don't say that out loud.

"No, I'm Russian and I don't have a lot of time before they notice I'm missing." The hairs on the back of my neck raise, my senses go into overdrive as the threat of danger becomes apparent.

"Who are you?" My voice is firm and leaves no room for argument.

"It doesn't matter, all you need to know is that he leaves the country for business in the Ukraine in four days. The only guards will be the four you work with and yourself at the house–"

"I only work at the club," I interject. I can't see her but I can picture her shaking her head.

"No, you will be moved to the house to make sure no one leaves." I lower my gun and straighten up as I stuff it back into my waistband.

"I don't understand what the hell you are saying?" I growl in frustration.

"Bring your computer man. He can get inside and find what he needs while you stand guard." I freeze but make sure to keep my shock from showing.

"I don't know what the hell–"

"I know everything, Gage Matthews, don't take me for a fool. You have four days to prepare your brothers and computer man. You won't get another chance like this."

"Who the hell are you and why should I believe you?" Anger laces each of my words. She finally steps into the light and fuck me, she is beautiful. Her blonde, shoulder length hair looks almost white. She has piercing blue eyes that remind me of the sky, wearing a blue sequined dress that hugs her curves in all the right places, and her legs, they are so long, the perfect length to wrap around my waist.

"If he ever found out I was here speaking with you, he would kill me." She moves forward until there is a small amount of space left between us and hands me an envelope, her eyes boring into mine. "If you tell anyone, even your brothers about the contents of that envelope, I'll make sure you never find it." With that said she turns to leave, going back toward the shadows but I call out, stopping her.

"Tell me your name," I demand. Her shoulders sag

slightly before she composes herself and holds her head high, continuing to walk back into the shadows. Before her silhouette can disappear from sight, she says so low I would have missed it if I hadn't been paying such close attention to her.

"My name is Anya Volkov."

Oh fuck!

I shake out of it and quickly head back around the front to my position. I'm on high alert now and can feel the tension radiating through my body. I just met the daughter of the Pakhan and she just gave me a way into his home. Can I trust her? I ponder over that thought as I discreetly open the envelope she gave me. It's a polaroid picture. I flip it over and everything inside me freezes, my heart skips a beat and everything begins to get hazy as I stare down at the picture in my hand. Chained like a dog to the wall, naked and bruised, looking so malnourished and dejected. Blood and dirt caked all over, chunks of hair missing, eyes that once seemed so bright and full of life are filled with nothing but pain.

"Rook," I whisper his name into the cold night like a prayer. He's alive and Anya-fucking-Volkov is going to help me get my brother back!

Chapter One

Gage

I can't go back to the house Bish and the others are holed up in, it's too risky in case someone is tailing me. I know they don't trust me yet and the Bratva isn't stupid. They have guards stationed at the hostel where all the *Shestyoka* stay. When I say all, I mean three of us. I am the only non-Russian but they don't know that. Each night I get here, shower and crawl into bed. I have no other choice. I don't trust these two to not spy on me and report back to the *captains*. Basically, I'm lowest of the low and they report to another low-level boss who tells me what to do. I'm nowhere near the action and need to find a way to climb this fucking ladder to get in with the captains.

I lay here staring up at the celling, sifting through my thoughts. I try to block out the image of Rook but it's fucking hard. I can't get the look in his eyes out of my head. I roll over and face the wall, not trusting that the other two are really asleep, and pull the photo of him I stuffed into the hole in the side of my mattress. I can see the bullet wounds on his chest, shoulder and arm. They've been stitched but with how filthy he looks, I'd be surprised if they don't get an infection.

I make a silent vow to myself that I will do whatever I have to in order to bring my brother home and I know who I need to help me make that happen. Anya Volkov may think she is untouchable and above me, but what she doesn't realize is I'm the worst out of all of my family. Unlike them, I won't go easy on her because she doesn't have a cock. She wanted to play with the big boys and knew exactly what she was doing when she gave me that photo, so I'll treat her like any other man. I'm going rogue here and deviating from the plan I have with my brothers and Vin. My first order of business is to find Anya. She is going to help me climb the ranks and get in close to her father. Once I take Vlad out, I'm going after Rook because there is no fucking way, I am leaving Russia without my baby brother.

I rub my hands together to try to keep warm. It's fucking freezing here and I hate it. I have so many layers of clothing on and I can still feel the chill of the night air all the way to my bones. Nothing ever happens here. I stand guard all night for fucking nothing. There is no action on this side of the club. I tried to work the front to get a look at who comes and goes but Krill, the guy I answer to, told me to fuck off and not come back around again. All that did was pique my interest. He doesn't want me at the front because I would see someone I shouldn't.

I pull the pack of smokes from my pocket and place one between my lips. As I light it, I inhale and the moment the nicotine hits my system I sigh and relax a bit. I don't smoke often, but every now and then I need something to take the edge off. I'm more tense and agitated lately since I haven't been able to fight since I landed in Russia nearly seven weeks ago. I flew separately from Bishop and the others, flying commercial so that if they tracked my movements, they would have a paper trail of me entering the country. I guess it worked. Down side is the moment I met with Krill, the fucker confiscated my passport.

"*Sobaka.*" comes through the radio. I have no fucking idea what that word means but it's what they call me around here. I take another drag of my cigarette before I grip my radio at my waist and answer.

"Da?" (*Yes*) I answer and wait for whoever it is to speak again.

"Prikhodite na front, seichas." (*Come to the front, now*) I'm getting pretty good at understanding Russian now, normally I stand out here with an ear bud in my ear and listen to *How to speak Russian for dummies.* The book sounds stupid but believe it or not, it's because of that book I understand what he is saying. It's fucking hard when they speak fast and I can't catch certain words.

"Vie puti," I say back as I drop my smoke and stomp on it before heading around the front. Nervous energy thrums through me. This is the first time I have ever been moved from my position unless it was to check a noise or follow an order. I slow my pace as I near the front, this could be a fucking trap and I'm walking right into it. I weigh my options and, in the end, I decide to hell with caution. I round the corner and I'm met by a long line of people waiting to get into the club. Girls stand there in skimpy dresses and heels acting like they aren't freezing their tits off when it's fucking snowing out. I shake my head and cut through the queue of people to get to the door.

As I near the door where the two large bouncers stand minding the red rope to keep the people back, the one with a scar above his eye nods as he motions for me to head inside. I keep the shock from my face and do as I'm told. I pull the door open and I'm immediately assaulted by the sound of the techno track that is playing. I probably should have asked them where the fuck do I go but I didn't want to give them a reason to tell me to fuck off and miss this chance to get a glimpse of the club. I move into the entryway of the club and out of nowhere two guys in black suits appear, I stiffen ready for them to throw hands.

"Lift your arms." The larger of the two guys steps forward, I lift my arms at my sides as he pats me down. He stops at my waistband, pulls my gun out and tosses it to his partner. He takes the blade strapped to my ankle and backup gun I have strapped to my other ankle. Once he's disarmed me, they take my coat and jumper then open a side door motioning for me to enter. I'm not mad they took my coats, it's fucking warm in here. The further I get down this dimly lit red corridor that has doors either side, my blood begins to circulate in my hands again and I start to feel the tips of my toes. What is it with Russian's and the fucking color red? I round the corner and come to a stop. So far, all the walls and doors are red except for the door I am currently staring at, it's black.

I roll my neck side to side and say fuck it once again to caution. I close the distance between me and this fucking ominous door, grip the handle and pray to fucking God I'm not walking into an ambush. I push the door open and walk in. It's pitch black in here. I close the door and feel for the light switch, flick it on expecting to find a gun pointed at my head. It's not a fucking gun, it's worse than a bullet.

"What are you doing here?" I grit out as I dart my gaze around the room making sure we are alone and this isn't some type of set up to get me killed.

"Helping you," she scoffs.

"Why the hell would you do that?" She sits there on the edge of the double bed that is covered in red silk. The door may be black but the inside of the room is littered with red everywhere. I know what this room is. It also confirms what I already knew, that the club is just a cover for their more nefarious business.

"Do you know why everything is red from the moment you enter the corridor?" I narrow my eyes wondering if she can read my fucking thoughts. I run my gaze over her skeptical as fuck, I don't trust this chick and I know she has ulterior motives. She keeps her head held high, uncaring that I'm checking her out, unlike last time she wears a pair of skin tight jeans, a blush-colored blouse with black boots. Her hair is curled and frames her face, her face which is caked with makeup. I don't know why girls wear that shit, they don't need it. All it does is hide their natural beauty.

"Nah, but I bet you're gonna tell me why," I deadpan. She inhales and her shoulders hunch slightly as her eyes take on a faraway look as if she is reliving a horrible memory.

"The dimly lit lights and the color make it harder for anyone to make out the blood stains. It saves on the cleaning bill, but if you look close enough you will still be able to see the remnants of blood from the girls who were strong enough to fight back."

Chapter Two

I push the dark memories back into the box inside my mind, I never dwell on those memories because if I did, they would consume and destroy my life. He has already taken everything from me and I refuse to allow him to take anything else from me. He can hurt my body but not my mind. I blink a couple times and refocus on Gage, the man is stunning in his own ruggish lumberjack looking way. His blond hair is tied into a man bun on the top of his head, his green eyes are sharp and assessing, a five o'clock shadow is present on his face. His long-sleeve shirt does nothing to hide the taut muscles beneath it, his jeans cling to him like a second skin. Gage Matthews is a beast of a man and must have balls of steel to think he can overturn the Bratva and make it out alive.

"Why am I here, Anya?" he asks. I slowly lift my gaze from his boots and trail a path all the way up his body until I meet his guarded stare. I uncross my legs and slowly climb to my feet. He can try to deny it all he wants but I know he is struggling not to run his gaze over me and appreciate the view. Unlike most girls, my ass and tits are natural. I've learned to use those assets to my advantage when persuading others to do my dirty work. All I had to do was flash a bit of cleavage to Shen and within five minutes he had Gage in here without anyone noticing.

"The timeline for Vlad has been changed. You will not be returning to the hostel tonight." His left eye twitches as he darts his gaze around the room for the fifth time. "There is no one else here, you will not be ambushed." He cocks a brow and gives me a condescending look.

"Forgive me if I don't take you at your word." I take three steps toward him, leaving a few inches of space between us as I gaze up at him, even with my boots on I only come up to his neck.

"You may not like me but if you and I are both to make it out of here alive, we are going to need to trust each other." I grind my teeth to try and calm the anger thrumming through me when he snorts and shakes his head.

"It's pretty hard to trust a fucking snake when they hand you a picture of your brother chained like a fucking animal." I school my features making sure he can't get a read on my emotions. I didn't like doing that to him but it was the only way. "Is he even alive?" he asks softly. I can see in his eyes he's scared to hear my answer.

I lie. "Yes, he's alive." Some of the tension eases in his shoulders and his hands finally unclench at his sides.

"What do you want from me and don't fucking lie, give it to me straight or you're on your own." I swipe my tongue across my bottom lip. His eyes zero in on the movement, sending a thrill through me. Gage may act unaffected by my presence but his eyes betray him. He is attracted to me and hates it.

"I want your help to overturn my father and kill my uncle." He eyes me warily. He's smart enough to know that isn't all I want.

"And, what else?" I hold his gaze as I say it out loud for the first time.

"I'll set your brother free and end the skin trade with the Americans if you help me take over as the Pakhan of the Volkov Bratva." His eyes widen to the size of plates, clearly that was not what he was expecting me to say.

"You want to run the Bratva?" The suspicion is his voice is clear, but he doesn't understand.

"Truth is, no I don't want to run things. You Americans don't understand how things are here. The Bratva isn't just some illegal mafia family, it *is* Russia. If I take over, I can change things and help my country... set all these girls free and reunite them with their families." His face morphs into surprise. Clearly he expected me to be in this for the money.

"There is no way any of these guys will allow a woman to lead. I've been here for nearly seven weeks and all these sick fucks see women as are a hole to stick their cock in whenever they want." I grind my teeth to control my temper. I fucking hate the double standards. Men can do as they like and get away with it. If women do the same, we are a whore or a gold digger.

"I'm not most women. Agree to my terms and I will help you get what you need on my father." He eyes me skeptically for a moment. I can see it in his green eyes he doesn't like this deal but he has no choice.

"I won't promise you anything. If we have to burn this whole organization to the ground to get what we want, then we will. If there is a way for us both to get what we want, then I will do that. Is that good enough for you?" His honesty is refreshing and really it's not like I have any other choice here. We are each other's only options.

"Yes," I say as I turn to leave out the back door. I pull the door open and peer back over my shoulder to face him only to find his eyes glued to my ass. *Men.* "We leave in an hour. Be out front and don't be late. You won't get this chance again." I don't wait for a reply as I close the door behind me.

I'm packing all the files and papers that I'll need while I'm staying at the house. I normally stay at my apartment down the road. With Vlad being out of the country, it means I need to be under protection. All that means is I get shipped to his house, which is in the middle of nowhere, with three or four guards. Vlad doesn't give a fuck about me—never has and never will. The only reason I'm still alive is because he thinks he can use me to get Katarina back. I paid the price for her freedom, still am, but knowing that he can't use her against me or sire another heir makes this all worth it.

"The car is ready." I look up from my desk and nod to Krill. He may look harsh and fucking scary but the truth is, he has saved my ass countless times. Krill isn't like most of the others. He doesn't enjoy hurting women or killing. He only does it because there is no way out of the Bratva— death is your only escape from this life.

"I'll be out in a minute." Krill nods as he closes the door. I gather everything I will need to work from Vlad's.

Everyone thinks being the Pakhan's daughter I have it easy, I really fucking don't. I handle all his books and oversee his accounts. If there is any error with his money it's me that is in the firing line. Vlad only cares about money, power and hurting his enemies.

I head out of my office—if you could call my Harry Potter sized room an office. It's so fucking tiny all that's in there is my desk, chair and printer. The filing cabinets are in Ivan's office and I avoid going in there as much as I can. I hate my piece of shit uncle and I hate that I'm the one that is always tasked with cleaning up his fucking messes. I lock my door behind me and hope like fuck Ivan is gone already, heading toward the exit ready to flee this place.

"Anya!" I freeze, of course I'm not that lucky.

"Da?" I answer as I keep my gaze on the door in front of me. Ivan is a sleazy pig and the fact we share blood doesn't stop him from making lewd remarks or looking at me like he wants a taste.

"You gonna be lonely out there by yourself?" I shiver but not in a good way. I feel him getting closer and brace myself for his unwanted touch. He grips my waist in a punishing hold. I fight the flinch that wants to break free. Ivan loves it when girls fight back, he's a sick fuck. He plasters himself against my back making sure I can feel how hard he is, and I fight the urge to gag, knowing all it will do is entice him to keep chasing after me. "I could tell your father you need me." A shudder tears through me when he licks the back of my neck. I try to pull free but his hold on me tightens and turns to bruising.

"Your car is waiting." I snap my gaze to the side and see Gage standing there with a blank look on his face. He's trying to shield his anger but I can see it in his eyes. Ivan thrusts his hips once more before stepping back, and I sigh in relief. I nod to Gage to lead the way. He pushes the door open for me and I don't wait around and get the hell out of here. Gage places a hand on the small of my back and leads me toward the car that is idling at the curb. I don't smack his hand away when I know I should because people can see. The truth is, I like the feeling of his hand on me.

Chapter Three

Gage

I sit in the backseat beside her while the two others that stay at the hostel with me drive and ride shotgun. I've been informed that Krill will be joining us later this evening at the house. None of us have been told where we are going and just to follow the GPS. Anya sits there with her head resting against the glass. I have no idea who the fucking old ass creep was with his hands on her but I could tell from how still she was, and the look of disgust on her face, that his touch wasn't welcomed.

It was by pure chance I stumbled upon them. I had to take a piss so I rushed back inside and that's when I saw her as I came out of the bathroom. I peer over at her from the corner of my eye and really take the time to look at her. She puts on a brave face but I can see there is so much she holds back. Is it because of fear? Fuck, does she fear her father or is she just a spoiled brat and angry because daddy said no to buying her a new Bentley? I don't like the idea of using her but right now, she is my only choice to get the information I need to take down her father. If it's a choice between using her or saving my family, there is no choice. She will be the first to go.

I try to take in my surroundings so that if I needed to, I can find my way back here. It's too dark out and not enough street lights on the back road for me to keep track. Each time I shift to get a glimpse at the GPS the fucker riding shotgun moves to block me, which just proves that they are here to spy on me. I need to remember that while I'm scoping out the house. I managed to race back to the hostel and grab my shit. I cleared everything out in case they toss the room while we are away. I can't leave anything to chance, too much is riding on me to fuck this up. Her phone rings, pulling me from my thoughts. She fishes it out of her purse and answers it.

"What?" Her tone is curt and swift. She listens intently for a moment before her face morphs into annoyance. She begins to speak in Russian but it's too quick for me to understand everything she is saying. Whatever it is has clearly pissed her off. "I'll find someone," she snaps in English before ending the call. "We need to head back to the Den, turn around," she snaps.

The driver spins the car around without question and does as she orders. I have no idea what the Den is. From the look in her face, it isn't a place she likes to visit which tells me it's somewhere I need to check out.

We pull outside what appears to be a nightclub on the outskirts of town. Unlike the club I have been working at, this one doesn't have a line or cars lining the street. It looks abandoned, the neon sign above the door reads Den. It flickers and looks like it's about to blow out.

"Park around back," Anya snaps. I peer over at her and notice she is more tense than before and a mask of indifference has slipped into place. We pull around the back to park and that's when I see all the cars. What the fuck is this place? We find a place to park and climb out. Anya heads straight to the trunk and pops it. She digs through her bag and grabs a few items of clothing before closing it again. She nods to the two fuckers and they lead the way—the fact they know where to go and how to get here proves to me that they are spying on me for intel.

I walk beside Anya, making sure to keep an eye out around me, this place should be easy enough to find again if I needed to. The closer we get to the door, I begin to hear the bass of the music and the roar of the crowd. I keep my face void of emotion as I feel Anya's gaze on me. The dimly lit back door is old and rusted with bits of paint peeling off it. Photos from google show Russia being beautiful and majestic but so far, the parts I have seen are anything but. Just as one of the dicks goes to grab the handle of the door, he stops when Anya speaks up beside me.

"Alexi, you man the door from the inside and Vor, you will accompany me and Gage to the back to prepare. Once it's over, we leave without delay." So that's their names, good to know. Each of them nod before Alexi pulls the door open for us. I pause when the sounds of a cheering crowd hits me, they're so loud the sound of them overpowers the music. I follow after Anya and Vor while Alexi stands guard at the door. I take in as much of my surroundings as I can while trailing after Anya, there must be over a hundred people packed into this makeshift bar. The stench of stale beer and smoke overwhelms me. I scrunch my nose in disgust and breathe through my mouth. Anya remains between me and Vor as he pushes his way through the crowd. I'm bumped and shoved as I make sure to keep her secure and safe between our bodies.

I shove some drunk out of the way and stumble to a stop, right there in front of me is what all this chaos is about. A cage stands in the middle of this place with two guys in the ring fighting, each of them looking like shit. Blood coats their bodies and one of them must have taken a good hit to the eye because it's swollen shut. I watch as the guy in the purple shorts advances and swings a right hook, the other guy in yellow dodges it, drops low, then swings an uppercut sending the guy in purple to his ass. Yellow jumps on top of the other guy and reigns down blow after blow. The other guy, who I assume is the ref, doesn't break them apart, even when it's clear the guy on the ground is unconscious.

He's not gonna stop.

"Come on, we don't have time." I pull my gaze from the murder happening in front of me to stare down at the blonde Russian. The pity in her eyes tells me she doesn't like this.

"They're all just gonna watch as he kills him?" The confusion in my voice can be heard above the cheers of the crowd. I'm jostled around but stand my ground. She reaches out and grips my hand leading me away from the fight. Just as we hit a hallway where two guys stand guard, I peer over my shoulder and that's when I see it, yellow shorts has his foot on the guys neck. He looks out to the screaming crowd as he raises his arms up smiling, twists his foot and snaps the guys neck sending the crowd into a bigger frenzy. What the fuck is this place?

She drags me down the corridor and stops at the second door on the right. She pushes it open and drags me inside. I see Vor leaning against the far wall with a scowl on his face. She kicks the door closed, then heads over to the lockers in the corner. She sits on the bench seat in front of the lockers and starts taking her boots off. I look to Vor, hoping he has some insight into what the hell she is doing but his gaze is fixed on her. I look back to see her undoing her blouse. I growl before moving in front of the pervert and blocking his view.

"Didn't your mother teach you that it's rude to stare?" His eyes narrow as he pulls his upper lip back in snarl. When the stench of his breath hits me, I fight to not gag. At least if he's standing here getting in my face, he isn't looking at her getting undressed. Wait, why the fuck is she undressing? I turn toward her, ready to demand some answers, but freeze. Her back is to us as she unclasps her bra and lets it topple to the ground before pulling a sports bra over her head. Her back is covered in ink. Two giant koi fish surround the outside of her back, in the center is little huts and some other things I can't make out, but the one thing that does stand out is the star in the center of her back marking her as part of the Russian Bratva. Seeing the star right there in the center has me clenching my fists at my sides and grinding my teeth. She may be Koby's best friend and beautiful as all hell, but I need to remember that she is the daughter of my enemy.

Chapter Four

I can feel his gaze on me. Unlike Vor's, it doesn't send a shiver of disgust through me. Vor is here to make sure that I don't take any weapons in the ring. Fucking asshole loves this part of his job, especially when he gets to pat me down even though he watched me change. Once my sports bra is on, I take a deep breath and begin to undo my jeans. I push them down and try to block out the fact that both of them are getting a good view of my thong-covered ass. The sharp intake of breath behind me lets me know it's Gage. It's not from seeing my ass though, it's from shock that my tattoo goes all the way to the bottom of my ass cheeks. I quickly grab my tights off the wooden bench seat and slip them on. I bend over and gather my hair into a high ponytail so it doesn't get in the way. Once that's done, I grab my sneakers and socks from my locker and drop down onto the bench to put them on.

"What the hell's going on?" I don't look at Gage as I continue to go about putting my shoes on, I don't have time to baby him or explain this as I'm up next.

"Vor, wait outside." He grunts his disapproval but does as I ask. I say nothing until the door closes behind him. "You stand ring side and do not intervene or try to help," I say to Gage as I stand and place everything neatly inside my locker. I reach around and undo the clasp of my necklace, then place a kiss on the gold cross and lay it on top of my clothes. It's the only thing I have of my mother's. I close my locker and roll my shoulders before cracking my neck side to side to get hyped for what's about to happen. Gage grips my arms, spins me around and slams me back against the lockers. He pins me with an angry scowl.

"What the fuck is going on?" I shove him back and duck when he tries to grab me again and dart into the corner where there is a small table set up with the tape I need for my hands. I turn back to Gage. I can see he's pissed and confused as fuck about what's happening but he will never understand this situation.

"You can either help me tape my hands or I call out for Vor. The choice is yours." I give him a few seconds. He just stands there staring at me, so I give up and open my mouth to shout for Vor but snap it closed when he growls and steps forward. He snatches the tape from me and begins to do as I asked, saying nothing until he finishes taping my first hand and moves onto the next.

"Why are you fighting?" This time his tone is just... confused?

"I disobeyed and now I have to prove I'm worthy

enough to live." He snaps his gaze to mine, his green eyes searching mine for a lie he won't find because it's the truth.

"Your father knows about this?" he asks as he finishes taping my hand. I step and call for Vor. He enters and comes straight for me, shouldering Gage out of the way. Gage holds my stare over Vor's shoulder as he pats me down. I focus on the color of Gage's eyes to distract me from the way Vor grasps my tits and cups my pussy. Gage's jaw stiffens as Vor lowers to his knees in front of me, his face perfectly in line with my pussy, neither of us missing the sound of his inhale. I fucking hate this prick and how he does that every time I have to fight. "She's fucking clean," Gage snaps as he yanks Vor back, causing him to fall to ass. Before they can get into it, I dart in between them and shoot each of them a warning look, before settling on Vor.

"Skazi im, chto ya gotov." (*Tell them I'm ready.*) Vor shoots me a scathing look but does as he's told like a good guard dog. He may hate it but even I'm ranked higher than he is.

"Answer my question!" Gage snaps as soon as Vor leaves the room. I look over at him from the corner of my eye and shake my head, he still doesn't get it.

"Who the fuck do you think gave the order?" I deadpan before I walk out of the room and prepare myself for the pain I'm going to be in. No pity is taken on me because of who my father is, Vlad has made it clear to everyone that I am free game. No one will pull their hits because I have tits. I don't get special privileges like not having to go through this or being exempt from punishment. I'm just like any other captain in the Bratva, except they are treated with respect and I'm not. I wait at the end of the corridor behind the two guards who will escort me to the ring. Everyone in here hates me because of who I am. It's the reason I'm made to fight here, because all of these assholes would love to watch me get my ass dragged out of here in a body bag. The announcer begins their spiel about a special main event, but I tune him out when I feel Gage step beside me.

"Which is the girl you're fighting?" I snort and shake my head while fighting to not laugh at his stupidity. I can feel his glare burning a hole into the side of my head, but I keep my gaze forward, not willing to allow him to distract me. I seem to forget my place whenever I look into his eyes and that is dangerous for both of us.

"Still not getting it, I see." The announcer says my opponent's name and the crowd cheers so loudly my ears begin to ring. Then when he says mine boos sound out, some of them even yell loud enough that I hear them calling me horrible things. I try to channel the anger inside me at what people presume of me, I need to use that anger to win this fight. Just as the guards step forward ready to lead me to the ring, I glance quickly over at Gage who is staring at me and say, "Women don't fight here, only men." His eyes widen but I don't stick around. I follow after the two guards who forge a path for me, the crowd shouting at me calling me a slut, whore—you name it they say it. One even shouts that they have prayed for my death. Truth is, I can't blame them for hating me. They throw cups of beer at me, water bottles, shoes. I duck when I see a glass bottle flying toward me. The next thing I know my head is pushed down and I'm being covered by Gage's body as he helps me to the ring.

The crowd goes nuts when I get to the opening of the cage. Vor stands there by the opening, nodding for me to enter. Just as I step through, Gage yanks me back. I shoot him a warning look. He can't stop this and if he tries to he will get the both of us killed. Vor steps forward to push

Gage away but he's too slow. Gage snakes out his arm and wraps his hand around Vor's throat holding him in place.

"Hold your guard up, listen to me from the ring side and I'll guide you. Don't strike first and stay on the defense until I get a read on his moves." I search his gaze for a second. When I see he is dead serious, I nod and step into the ring when he releases me. It's as if I've stepped into a sound-proof room as soon as the gate is closed and locked behind me, everything went silent. That door won't be unlocked until one of us isn't breathing. I take in my opponent, Andreas the announcers called him. He's tall and lean, not skinny lean but more like toned and muscle lean. The guy stands at least a couple feet taller than me, his head shaved and covered in tattoos. His whole body is, but when my eyes land on the tattoo over his chest, my blood turns to ice.

Voron.

He's a fucking Crow! A smile stretches across his face when he realizes I now know he belongs to the Crows. The Crows were nothing but a group of wannabes that could never make it in the Bratva. Over the years they grew in numbers and have since caused nothing but problems for us. They used to be nothing more than a thorn in our sides but now, they have amassed an army of their own with loyal followers. The Crows hate what we stand for and want to kill us on sight. I have never really had much to do with them and have only heard the stories from some of the other Bridgers and Captains. I'm pulled from my inner turmoil when the ref shouts for us to fight. Unlike normal fights, there is no rounds in this one, you keep fighting until one of you is dead. I say a silent prayer to whoever is listening to help me get through this fight and let me live to see another sunrise.

Chapter Five

Gage

The guy, Andreas I gather is his name since the crowd hasn't stopped chanting it, charges toward her. She looks regal and deadly—black sports bra and skin tight black tights, her hair piled on top of her head. Her face is blank of all expression, she is doing an amazing as fuck job at keeping the fear off her face. Andreas throws a right hook. She ducks and jumps away from him. His reach is longer than hers and he's quicker on his feet, she needs to use her small size to her advantage and keep tiring him out, then it's time for her to go on the attack. She dodges his left hook only for him to strike out with a one-two combo and land a right jab to her ribs. She stumbles a few steps until her back is against the cage, the smirk on his face says it all, she needs to move before he pins her there.

"Get the fuck off the cage!" I yell. She flicks her gaze to me quickly before managing to just miss his leg coming up to connect with her head. My mouth drops open in shock when she grips his leg while it's still in the air using her right shoulder to support the weight of it as she begins to land blow after blow to his midsection. He tries to hit her back but can't get his balance while hopping on one leg. He does manage to land a jab right in the center of her face. She screams out in pain but doesn't drop to the ground and weep like I thought she would. Blood gushes from her nose and trails down her chin. She switches it up and stomps down on his foot while pushing the other one higher.

His eyes bug out of his head as he grits his teeth in pain the further she stretches his leg up. He uses all his strength to throw her off but she doesn't budge. The girl is a lot stronger then she looks. Pushing his leg above her head, he roars in pain, then swings out landing a right hook to the side of her face. She stumbles to the side dropping her hold on his leg. Each of them are breathing hard and take a split second to rest before she says fuck caution and charges at him, wrapping her arms around his waist and tackles him to the ground. They grapple on the floor rolling around the ring fighting for the top spot, each of them landing hits to the other. I fucking hate standing here like a bitch watching this fucker hit a woman right in front of me.

"Switch directions and use your fucking legs!" I scream over the roaring crowd, who is yet to stop chanting the fucker's name. She must hear because he tries to roll right but she leans left, stopping his momentum then continues to rain down hit after hit until he bucks his hips and throws her off balance. In the next second he's on top of her. She holds her hands over her face guarding it. That doesn't stop him—the coward has a woman half his size pinned beneath him and still continues to find a way to hurt her. He starts punching her chest. I grind my teeth in anger as I grip the chain link fence shaking it. She needs to move or he'll shatter her fucking collarbone! "You need to fucking move!" I yell.

She tries to break left but he's too heavy for her to move, bucking her hips but he doesn't shift an inch.

Fuck!

I can see her trembling from the pain, I move to the gate to go and get her the fuck out of there before he kills her. I'm two steps from the gate when Vor blocks my path seething with anger.

"Get the fuck out of my way!" I growl, not even trying to fake a Russian accent now and by the look on his face it doesn't seem like he noticed.

"You try to help, she dies." He may be a sick fuck but I can see it in his eyes he doesn't like her being in there either.

"We have to do something," I grit out as I peer around and manage to catch Anya striking out with a solid jab to the cunt's nose. The impact disorientates him and she uses that to her advantage. She lifts her hips and turns, throwing him off her. She crawls away and uses the cage to help her to her feet, her face is covered in blood, her chest and abdomen are already starting to bruise. She clutches her right side and winces. Andreas is on his hands and knees now, so she rushes forward and kicks him right in the face. I push past Vor and grip the cage watching her. She keeps the pain she feels from showing on her face as she continues to kick and stomp his face. The final blow is when she jumps in the air and lands her knee right on his cock. He shoots into a sitting position screaming in agony, the roar of the crowd turns to shocked gasps. She jumps to her feet, spins and kicks him right in the face, knocking the fucker out.

She jumps on top of him, punching and smacking his face. I furrow my brow when she drops her right hand to her waistband, faking that she is holding her injured side before she pulls her hand back and... covers his mouth. Is she planning on suffocating him? She keeps her hand on his mouth as she uses her left hand to wrap around his neck. A moment later, she uses both her hands to strangle the life from him, then she throws her head back and screams. Her scream is filled with rage, pain and... agony for what she is doing. A minute passes by before she rolls off and shuffles back on her ass, staring at his lifeless body. The ref rushes over and places two fingers against his pulse, the crowd quiet as they wait for the official call. The ref darts his gaze to Anya and gives her a curt nod. I watch as all the air rushes from her body.

One of the guards that led us out here, steps forward and unlocks the gate. The second it's open, I charge through and head right for her. I crouch down in front of her and gently cup her face. She winces in pain. I peer over my shoulder when a couple of other guys enter the cage and watch as they carry the fucker's body out. Unlike the last fight, the crowd isn't cheering at the death of this man. They are booing and throwing shit at the cage. I swivel so I can lift her and carry her out, but she bats my hands away and pushes me back.

"I'm walking out of here," she says with such conviction I don't argue, instead I help her climb to her feet. She stands tall and holds her head high. I can tell it's causing her pain but she refuses to look weak in front of all these people. I follow after her. Vor is at the door waiting and ready to clear a path for her. The crowd shouts and throws things but she keeps her head up acting like they don't bother her. When we reach the entrance of the corridor, one ballsy fucker steps forward and spits right in her face. I act without thinking. I punch the cunt right in the face and bask in my glory when his eyes roll back and he drops to the ground like a sack of shit. I place my hand on the small of her back ushering her forward. Vor opens the locker room door for us and closes it once we're inside.

"You have twenty minutes," he snaps from the doorway. She nods her head and limps toward her locker. I rush forward ready to help her anyway I can, to try ease some of her pain but she pins me with a look that tells me everything she can't say. If Vor sees me taking pity on her and helping her it makes her look weak and also calls into question what type of relationship I have with the Pakhan's daughter. I nod stiffly before claiming my position against the wall standing guard. It fucking sucks standing here watching her struggle to change. A small whimper sounds from her when she lifts her arms above her head to take off her sports bra. I cut a glance to Vor, unlike before he isn't staring at her like he wants to eat her. His gaze is focused on his shoes. She's earned his respect from winning that fight.

Chapter Six

Anya

The car ride passed by in a blur to Vlad's house. My whole body aches and my head is pounding with a headache that has my eyes watering. All I want to do is go inside, take some painkillers, shower and crawl into bed with a bottle of vodka to help numb the pain. I should have fucking known Ivan wouldn't have let me get away with blowing him off the way I did. I really didn't think he would call Vlad and snitch. When the Pakhan issues an order, you have no choice but to follow it or you wind up six feet deep. Vlad had to have known Andreas was fighting tonight. He was hoping the Crows would get their pound of flesh through me and stop fucking up his business.

Alexi pulls the car to a stop in front of the gothic style house. I can't bring myself to even bathe in its beauty.

This house used to bring such joyful memories but that was all a mirage. As soon as Vlad brought Katarina and I home from the States, I saw who my father was for the first time. He is a nightmare dressed as a daydream. I don't wait for anyone to open my door, I push it open and grit my teeth through the pain as I climb out of the car using the door as a crutch. The front door swings open to reveal Mora, the butler that lives here full time. I leave the guys to grab the bags as I make my way inside and head straight for the liquor cart in the living room. I pour myself a glass of vodka and slam it back relishing in the burn. I pour myself another before heading to my room, telling Mora to bring me some pain pills on my way past. He doesn't even bat an eye at my appearance, after all the years he has been with my family he has seen worse, much worse.

Once inside my room, I start to unbutton my blouse trying not to hiss in pain with each movement. A knock sounds at my door and I call for Mora to come in, keeping my back to him. Except, it isn't Mora. Gage steps in front of me and I grip my blouse holding it together.

"What the hell are you doing in here?" I demand. He searches my face and I hate the look of pity I see in his eyes. He says nothing as he holds out a glass of water and two white pills in the palm of his hand. "You really think I'm gonna trust you and just take those?" He sighs tiredly and shakes his head.

"The butler gave them to me when I told him I was bringing you your bags." In too much pain to argue, I take the risk and trust what he says, popping the pills in my mouth, then taking the glass from him and downing it before giving it back to him.

"Close the door on your way out," I say as I try with all my might not to limp toward my bathroom—Andreas got me good with a solid kick to my thigh. My whole body aches with pain… shit even the strands of my hair are painful. I hobble over to my bath and lean down to put the plug in. I cry out in pain when a searing pain shoots down my side and robs me of my breath. An arm wraps around my waist. I jolt in shock and instantly regret it when another sharp pain ricochets through me.

"Just let me fucking help you." Gage sounds pissed and I don't understand why, I'm not his concern and he shouldn't be in here. If Vor or Alexi were to see him in my room, Vlad would personally dish out my punishment for this act of disobedience.

"You can't be in here," I grit out as he ushers me back to lean against the counter while he starts the bath for me.

"And you shouldn't have been in that cage." I glare at his back as he leans over the tub to test the temperature of the water.

"Some of us don't have the luxury of getting to pick and choose what we want to do." I hear the bitterness in my own voice. He slowly turns toward me and I notice the pitying look in his eyes is replaced by determination.

"Help me do what I need to and I promise you, you will never have to do anything like you did tonight again."

"You say the sweetest things," I say mockingly.

"I mean it."

"I know you do and that is where we differ. Unlike you, I don't have my head in the clouds. I know I don't have a chance at life where I have a family or a man that adores me. I am Anya Volkov, heiress to the Volkov Bratva and that means I will be fighting for my life daily, until someone eventually gets the drop on me and puts me down." I don't even look at him, I'm not willing to see the sad look on his face. I release my hold on my blouse and shrug it off. Hissing, I hear him growl before he is crowding me again and helping me pull it the rest of the way off.

"Let me fucking help you at least." I want to argue but truth is, I really do need his help, so I nod stiffly. He crouches down in front of me and pops the button on my jeans. I suck in a sharp intake of air as he slowly pulls my zipper down. Gage lifts his gaze to mine as he grips the belt loops of my jeans and slowly peels them down my legs. For some unknown reason this moment feels so intimate just from the way he is looking at me. I step out of my jeans. He remains crouched in front of me for what feels like hours but is mere minutes before he slowly stands. We're so close that his chest brushes against my bra as he stands. I have to crane my neck back to keep eye contact with him. He slowly reaches around my back and unclasps my bra, drawing a gasp from me. He never takes his eyes off mine as he slowly brushes the straps off my shoulders and steps back just enough for my bra to drop to the floor in front of us.

"I can't–" I begin to say before he cuts me off.

"I'm gonna help you out of your tiny ass thong. I want to promise you that I won't look, but I also don't want to lie to you." He has done nothing aside from help me undress and just be... kind, but his words and the tenderness of his touch and willingness to help me without expecting me to get on my knees, has me growing wet. I dart my tongue to moisten my lips. His eyes track the movement and I nibble down on my bottom lip warring within myself. I shouldn't allow him to see me bare like this, but this other part of me wants him to drop to his knees and worship me. God, what would it feel like to have his mouth on my pussy? "Keep looking at me like that and we're gonna have a problem." I blink a few times to clear my thoughts. He quickly steps back and turns the bath off before reclaiming his position again.

"I think I can take it from here." The breathy tone of my voice has me cringing, I need to get my shit together. A small smirk pulls at the corner of his mouth as he slowly lowers in front of me, this time, he doesn't keep his eyes on mine. He takes a good look at my tits on his way down. I bite my lip to keep myself from moaning at the hungry look in his eyes. His face is an inch from my pussy as he grips the thin strings at my sides and slowly begins to pull them down. I pray that he doesn't see the wet spot on my panties. He follows the trails of my panties down my legs and just as I lift my left leg out of them, an animalistic sound comes from him. I look down to find his gaze transfixed on the crotch of my panties. He snaps his gaze to mine and the lustful look in his eyes has my breath lodging in my throat.

"You wet for me, Anya?" The neediness in his voice has me opening and closing my mouth several times, but no words come out. His eyes bore into mine for a moment before he tears his eyes from mine to stare at my freshly waxed pussy. A shiver runs down my spine when he darts his tongue out to moisten his lips. I attempt to clench my thighs together but he moves so fast. His hands grip my thighs gently to not cause me any more pain as he runs his nose up and down my slit inhaling.

"Mmmm, you smell fucking amazing." I moan in response, this is the most intimate moment of my life—no one has ever gone down on me before. He gently lifts my uninjured leg and hoists it over his shoulder. He cuts his gaze to mine, the green of his eyes seem to have darkened. "Tell me now if you want me to stop." I shake my head which just brings a broad smile to his face. He swipes his tongue through my folds, drawing a sharp cry from me. He does it again as he feels around on the floor for something. I watch as he grips my panties, lifts his arm up and pushes them inside my mouth as his tongue starts to lick my cunt. "You spit those out, I stop. Keep fucking quiet before the goon squad comes rushing in here." I am eagerly ready to agree to whatever he wants if he just keeps eating me.

He parts my lips with his fingers, exposing my intimate part, groaning at the sight and a sense of pride swells inside me. Gage pushes his tongue inside my hole. I rise up on my toes, shocked by the intense feeling. He uses his other hand to grip my ass holding me in place as he continues to fuck me with his tongue. He switches his tongue for a finger and sucks my clit into his mouth, my cries are muffled by my panties. I'm thankful for his forethought with trying to keep me quiet. I can't pull my gaze from him, watching him finger me and eat my pussy like it's the most delicious thing he's ever tasted is so fucking hot. I reach up and twirl my nipples between my fingers moaning at the sensations thrumming through me. He inserts two fingers inside me and picks his pace up, I pinch my nipples and feel my pending orgasm getting closer. He swipes his tongue over my clit twice before he sucks it into his mouth again, pulling my orgasm from me. I throw my head back and scream out my release. He doesn't stop fingering me or sucking on my clit until a pressure builds inside my pussy, only then does he yank his fingers free as I squirt all over the floor.

Chapter Seven

Gage

Fuck that was hot!

I stare up at her with a shit eating grin on my face, her cheeks are flushed and her eyes are glassy from her orgasm. I fucking knew she would be a squirter! I gently lift her leg from my shoulder and stand, my cock is rock fucking hard and begging me to burying it deep inside her tight wet hole. Her eyes slowly start to focus again as I reach out and pull her panties from her mouth. Her eyes search mine but I don't give her time to find what she is looking for. I lead her toward the bath carefully, maneuvering her around her... puddle. I hold her forearm as she climbs in the bath slowly, only letting go when she is seated under the water. I turn away from her, grab a towel from the corner and clean up our mess. I chuck the towel and her clothes in the hamper in the corner before I turn back to her.

"I'm gonna go get set up, then I'll come back and help you out of the tub." She says nothing, just nods her head. I head out and go to my room which is two doors down from hers. I close the door behind me and lean my head against it. What the fuck was I thinking? Seeing her standing there in nothing but her bra and panties had me thinking fuck my mission, I need to taste her. I push off the door and scrub a hand down my face. I need a cold shower and to wash the taste of her out of my mouth. She tastes so fucking sweet, her pussy fucking beautiful. I could sit crouched in front of her for hours just staring at it.

"Fuck," I snarl into the empty room as I strip off and head for the shower. I turn it to freezing cold but it does nothing to snap me out of my thoughts of her and the way she tasted. Fuck, when she came, she squeezed the fuck out of fingers and I'm standing here with my cock in my hand wondering what it would feel like if it were my cock inside her and not my fingers. I take a deep breath through my nose and regret it instantly when the musky smell of her pussy assaults my senses. I grip my cock and pump it once, hissing. I press my other hand against the tiled wall of the shower as I continue to pump my cock. Images of her perfect tits and her dusty pink nipples flash inside my mind. I groan at the thought of sucking and biting down on each of them as she writhes beneath me, screaming my name as I pound inside her tight little body.

I quicken my pace as I picture her naked on my bed, legs spread open waiting for me to fuck her any way I want. I bite down on my lip to quieten the sounds coming from me, feeling my balls begin to tighten and I come so fucking hard to thoughts of her. My cum spurts over the tiled wall. I slump forward, resting my head against it as I wait for my breaths to even out. One fucking taste of her isn't going to be enough. I never should have allowed myself to touch her because now, all I want to do is touch her, taste her and fuck her. I can't let my want for her derail me from what is important, even if her pussy is the best I've ever fucking tasted.

After dressing in some sweats and a shirt, I make my way back to her room. I make sure no one is watching when I slip inside her room and quietly close the door behind me. I make my way to her bathroom only to find her standing in the middle of the room with a towel wrapped around her, her hair wrapped in a towel as well. I frown at her before closing the space between us and gripping her arm as I lead her back into her room.

"What the hell are you doing?" she snaps.

"I told you to wait for me, you could have fucking slipped on the tiles and in your state, you wouldn't have been able to break your fall." I turn her and crowd her space until the backs of her legs hit her bed, she gently sits down, winces a couple times but doesn't make a sound. Her face is free of blood but bruises cover most of the surface, her chest is also black and blue. I clench my hands into fists at my side and grind my teeth in anger. What fucking twisted fucker could do this to a woman?

"It's worse than it looks," she says quietly as she grips my hand in one of her tiny ones. I shake my head denying her claim.

"Don't bullshit me. I fight for a living, Anya. I run the fight scene back home and there is no fucking way I would have let that fight happen tonight at my gym." Her eyes soften as she gazes up at me, a small smile lifts the corner of her mouth.

"I would love to visit this place you described. The school I was at in America was just as bad as it is here."

"Why the fuck would you want to stay here then? If you help me do this–" She leaps from the bed so fast ignoring her pain as she clamps a hand over my mouth. Her eyes are wide with fright as she shakes her head and leans forward, I lean down so she can whisper in my ear.

"The bath was running before to hide our conversation, the walls in this house have ears Gage. You need to watch what you say because I assure you, someone is always listening and you have already said too much." I want to blame it on the fact that I am still riding the high of my own orgasm but the truth is, I just want to see her reaction.

"So, you mean your father was probably listening to me get myself off in the shower to thoughts of his little girl?" She gasps and reels back in shock, her flushed cheeks, wide eyes and the way her mouth parts slightly, has a small chuckle escaping me. "You need help to change?" She nods but the move seems robotic. She tells me which drawers to grab clothes out of, once I have everything, I dump them on the edge of the bed as she drops her towel. This time, I don't stop for a snack as I help her into her lace panties and sleep shorts. She hisses and flinches as I help her into her shirt and my anger spikes all over again.

"Tomorrow, Vor and Alexi have to head back to town for a few hours, you will have about forty minutes to do what it is you need to before Krill arrives." I nod my head. "Vlad's office is on the second floor, third door on the right. I'll distract Mora while you do your thing. You need to be fast, Gage. If you're caught, I won't be able to help you. You won't be able to bring your brothers in. I thought the place would be empty, I was wrong."

"Who else is here besides the butler?"

"There are always guards stationed at the gate round the clock, four more patrol the grounds but none of them come inside the house unless called for. He has a separate security system in his office, the code was Katarina's birthday but it has been years since I have been in there. If the alarm sounds, all the guards will be notified and so will Vlad and the other captains." Well fuck, that makes this whole thing a hundred times fucking harder to accomplish. I'm not like Knight and can't hack. He and Vin could probably crack the code in five seconds, me on the other hand, I suck at that type of shit.

"How long do I have before the alarm sounds?" The uneasy look on her face tells me I'm not going to like her answer.

"You have thirty seconds from the moment you open the door." I curse beneath my breath. Vlad is a paranoid motherfucker to have a separate alarm system for his office. One thing is clear though, for him to be that paranoid means everything I need is in that office. I'm taking a huge risk here. If I'm caught, I'm dead. If I don't do this, I lose the only chance we may have at taking him down for good. "If you trigger the alarm, the whole house will go into lock down and there will be no way out. This is the only chance you will have. After Vlad returns, my cousin will be staying here."

Nodding my head, I hold her gaze as I speak. "I do this, I get the intel I need and we take your father down and replace you as the head of the Bratva, you give me Rook." For a nano second, her eyes shift and I tense. I'm good at reading people, really fucking good and the shift of her eyes just now, tells me she is hiding something. I grip her arms and yank her to me, she flinches in pain but I don't give a shit. I bend so I'm right in her face, she tries to hold her composure, but it falters. "Tell me the fucking truth, where is my brother?"

She tries to pull free but I tighten my hold, not caring that I'm hurting her. "I told you, give me what I want and I'll give you your brother but not before then!" I release her with a hard shove. She stumbles back and catches herself on the edge of the bed, giving me a filthy look.

I eye her up and down with disgust. "You fuck me over, Anya, and I will take away the thing you want most in this world, don't fucking push me!" I spit out as I storm from her room, uncaring if I'm caught by any of the other guards. Right now, I could use a fucking fight to take my frustration out on someone. That girl is a mind fuck. She got under my skin tonight and I can't allow that to happen again.

Chapter Eight

Sitting at the breakfast counter sipping my coffee has me feeling all types of emotions. I used to sit up here and watch my mother bake shortbread cookies for Christmas. We would decorate them, then leave them out for Santa on Christmas Eve. I hate that I don't have many memories of her, I was seven when she died of some unknown illness. I was stupid to believe that lie. I know deep down inside of me that Vlad had her killed. He only married her out of duty to the Bratva. He never loved my mother, just needed her to make him an heir and even then she failed. There were complications when she gave birth to me. I was too young to understand why but I got a hold of her medical file a couple years ago and found out she had to have an emergency hysterectomy. She would never be able to carry another child–a son. Therefore, she was now useless to Vladimir and there was no reason to keep her around any longer. I'm surprised he even let her live for seven years after my birth.

I push away those memories when I hear the back door open and close. Footsteps sound out in the living room and I wait for whoever it is to come to me. Since Vlad isn't here, I'm in charge and every one of these assholes hate it. Vor, Alexi and Krill stalk into the kitchen with grim looks on their faces. I straighten on my stool and keep my *don't fuck with me* mask in place. All of these men that surround me daily see me as a cold-hearted bitch. I like it that way as it keeps them on their toes and me out of their fantasies.

"Vyplyunut ego," (*Spit it out.*) I snap. Vor and Alexi both look to Krill, waiting for him to say whatever it is that has them looking like they swallowed a lemon.

"We need you to pack a bag and be back in the city tonight." I eye Krill warily. He won't hold my gaze, which can only mean one thing. Out of the three of them, Alexi is the one I don't trust. Krill and Vor may leer and enjoy patting me down but I know they hate it when Vlad lays down the law and punishes me. Each of these men has tried to shield me from it, they can't stop it though and we all know it.

"Alexi, find Gage and bring him to me," I bark. He looks to the other two, who refuse to pay him any mind. He mumbles under his breath as he stomps from the room like a spoiled child not getting their way. I give a minute before I focus back on the two guards in front of me. I may trust them but not enough to divulge any of my secrets as at the end of the day, they still work for Vlad. "Why does he want me back?"

Vor drops his gaze to the floor. Krill doesn't cower,

instead he meets my stare as he speaks. "You have another fight tonight." My eyes widen in surprise, Vlad has never made me fight two nights in a row. I'm still fucking hurting from the beating I took from Andreas, there is no way I will make it out of that cage tonight. I know it and by the looks on both the guys faces, they know it as well. Today is going to be my last day. I'm not going to fucking waste it sitting here with these assholes.

Resigned to my fate I stand and place my mug on the counter, then pat Krill on the shoulder as I pass by. His shoulders hunch but I don't need his pity. I do the same to Vor but before I can pass by, he grips my wrist. I halt, looking from him to the grip he has on my wrist. His eyes search mine, I can see the struggle in his gaze. He wants to help me but he doesn't know how—he can't help, no one can.

"My life was never my own," I say in a firm tone, proud that my voice doesn't waiver. "At least this way I can go out swinging and say I fought to the very end." Vor takes a shuddering breath, his eyes close for a couple seconds, and when they open again, they shine with guilt and pity. I shoot him a sad smile and slowly pull out of his hold. I appreciate their sympathy but it won't help me. No matter what, even with all these injuries, I'll fight until my dying breath tonight.

I shove my runners into my bag and double check to make sure I have everything inside that I will need for the fight before zipping it closed. My bedroom flies open, banging against the wall. I spin around in fright nearly losing my footing but manage to catch myself at the last second on the edge of the bed. Gage stands there glaring at me, his chest is rising and falling rapidly, hands clenched into fists at his sides.

"You are not fighting tonight!" he grits out through clenched teeth. I sigh as I run a hand through my hair, bloody mafia men think they speak and we all bow to their commands. I turn my back to him, effectively dismissing him as I finish packing my bag. My duffle is yanked from my grasp and thrown across the room. I turn around and gasp. He's right there. He's so close my chest is against his, I have to crane my neck all the way back to see his face.

"What is the–" I'm cut off when his hand wraps around my throat and he shoves me back on the bed. Before I can even process what the hell happened, he is on top of me. He straddles my legs keeping them in place. I grit my teeth as I swing out and manage to land a solid left hook to his jaw. His head swings to the side and I smile victoriously up at him. A growl tumbles from his chest before he strikes out gripping my wrists in his hands and pinning them above my head. I thrash beneath him, bucking my hips and trying to roll side to side but he doesn't budge. "Get the hell off me!" I shout. His eyes narrow to slits as he bends down getting right in my face, his lips skim mine as he speaks.

"You are not fighting tonight." A shiver runs down my spine as memories of what those lips felt like on my skin race through my mind. I shake away the thoughts, not needing to be distracted while he is this close to me. Gage is a distraction I don't need and can't afford to have. Sadness enters his gaze, making all the fight flee my body as I stare up at him. His grip on my wrists loosens and I pull my hand free and cup his cheek. His features soften at my touch, this moment begins to feel so intimate and I don't know how to feel about that. "Why are you fighting? You're in no condition to go a single round with a kid let alone a grown ass man." The concern in his voice confuses me. Last night he wanted to strangle me and today he's tender and caring like a lover would be.

I smile sadly up at him. Gage is beautiful in a ruggedly handsome way, he doesn't even need to try to look a certain way to be noticed. "I don't have a choice," I answer honestly. "I was never supposed to make it out of that cage last night." His eyes harden and his body tenses above me. "Vlad needs me gone for some unknown reason. He can't outright kill me himself, so he needs it done publicly so there are witnesses."

His eyes search mine trying to decipher what is running through my mind. God, the first man that I find that doesn't give a shit about who I am, or is too scared to make a move because of who my father is, finally comes into my life and I have to give him up before I even have a chance to see where this thing between us goes. I hate that this is the life and family I was born into—but you can't choose your family.

"How long do we have before you have to leave?" I furrow my brow confused by his sudden change in demeanor.

"We need to leave here by five tonight. Why?" He scrambles off me and I quickly sit up, flinching slightly as I scoot to the edge of the bed, watching him pace. He stops every so often, looks at me, then shakes his head before continuing. He keeps this up for at least five minutes. I grow tired of watching him wear a hole in my bedroom floor, so I open my mouth ready to ask him what the hell is going on, but he just turns and stalks out of my room. I stare at the open doorway for a good minute before I snap myself out of my stupor and return to packing my bag, trying to distract myself from Gage's strange as fuck behavior.

Chapter Nine

Gage

I sit in the back seat, next to Anya, lost in my own thoughts. I should be celebrating and feeling like I'm on cloud-fuck-ing-nine that I managed to get into Vlad's office undetected. Luck must have been on my side because Koby's birthdate was still the fucking code! I won't lie, I was dropping my nuts the whole time and had a cold sweat dripping down my back. I managed to get in and out without anyone notic-ing. Knight and Vin will have been alerted the moment I plugged the key logger in, and I managed to plant a bug under his desk as well so they will be able to listen in on any conversations or meetings he has in there. I made sure to reset the alarm and lock the door on my way out, even wiping the handle down, just being extra cautious.

Vlad's office is a mess. How the guy can work in that or

even find anything is a mystery to me. I was dodging stacks of papers, files and God knows what else just to get to his desk. He has live in staff and yet he doesn't even trust them enough to clean his office. A part of me feels like it was almost too easy to get in and out without being caught. Nothing in my life has ever come easy. I've fought for everything I have, literally. So, to be able to get into his office and out without being found out doesn't really sit well with me. I'm pulled from my thoughts when a loud sigh escapes Anya. I lull my head to the side to see she is gazing out the window. Vor sits behind us while Alexi and Krill ride up front. I don't see the point in her having her own guards if all Vlad wants is for her to die, it makes no sense to me.

I stare at her in wonder. She may look like she lives a lavish lifestyle being the Bratva heiress but that couldn't be further from the truth. At first glance she looks the part, wearing all designer clothes, her hair is always styled perfectly and her makeup is on point. She is the image of perfection. The way she conducts and holds herself, you would never know that she is suffering or fighting to stay alive daily. This girl isn't what I expected, she is so much... more. My attention is pulled from her when we pull into the same carpark from last night, except tonight, it's packed and there isn't an empty spot insight. I sit forward and look out the window. People loiter in the lot, all their gazes are on the us, allwhile the blacked-out SUV rolls through the lot.

"They know you are fighting tonight." Krill's ominous tone fills the small space, he doesn't stop the car until we are in front of the door, which has a line nearly a mile long by the looks of it. I turn to Anya to gauge her reaction to this. I expected to see her freaking out or silently crying but instead, I find her putting her Air Pods in each ear and scrolling through her phone to find a playlist before she hits play. Krill and Alexi both hop out. I follow after them, then the sound of the gathering crowd's boos and shouts hit me. I grind my teeth together as I make my way around the car to her side. I shove Alexi out of the way as I help her out and wrap my arm around her ready to tuck her into my side. She pulls free of my hold, straightens and ignores the people around her, taunting and shouting for her death. Krill leads the way through the crowd as Alexi and I stand at her sides and Vor covers her back. The head phones make sense now, she knew they would be shouting and wanted to block them out.

It is taking everything inside me not to grab her and run out the back door. Unlike last night when we were here, I don't turn away like the other three. I stand here and watch as she strips down. Bruises cover her body and she tries to hide her pain, but I can see it on her face with every move she makes. I don't miss the slight flinch when she changes her bra for her sports one or even when she bends to change from her jeans into her spandex shorts. She reaches up to tie her hair and sucks in a sharp intake of air, her ribs are hurting her but she refuses to acknowledge the pain.

"You standing there judging me isn't helping anything." Her voice is firm and laced with anger but it isn't directed at me. She's pissed her own father is doing this to her and I can't blame her. I close the space between us not giving a fuck if the others see, but keep a couple inches of space between us. Her blue eyes sear me, begging me not to try and intervene. I release a long exhale as I scrub a hand down my face, at a loss as to what the fuck I am supposed to do here.

"Is there any way out of this?" I ask, barely above a whisper. Her gaze softens as a tender smile graces her beautiful face.

"No. This is how it has to play out. This is my life, Gage." I hate that she isn't fighting this. She should be running for the hills but she isn't. A part of me respects that but another part of me fucking hates it. Why I'm so strung out over this, I have no fucking idea. I've tried to tell myself it's because she is a woman and shouldn't be subjected to something fucked up like this, but I can't even lie to myself. Ever since arriving here in Russia and getting inside the Bratva, I have done nothing but look into each member. I started looking into who Anya Volkov was since I met her that first night. I've stared at a picture of her I managed to snag the night she left the club for hours—meeting her for the first time and seeing her beauty up close was something else. Pictures don't do her justice. Her strong will and stubbornness only add to my already growing attraction.

"You're not ready for another fight, I can't let you do this." Her brows pull together confused. "If my plan A doesn't work then I'm going to plan B but that means I can't give you what you want in the end," I say low enough for only us to hear. Both plans mean I blow my cover inside the Bratva and fuck everything up, but I can see my redemption in her eyes which makes what I have to do worth it.

"Time to strap up." We step apart at the sound of Krill's voice. I move out of his way when he steps in front of Anya and begins to strap her hands. Once Krill is done and steps aside, Vor makes his way toward her to pat her down. I shoot him a scathing look in warning. He kneels down in front of her and I wait for him to cup her sex or inhale her scent but... he doesn't. It's as if in the past twenty-four hours everyone in this room except Alexi has grown some form of respect for each other.

"She's clear," Vor announces as he climbs to his feet and steps aside, then motions for her to head out. I close my eyes for a second to gain control of my emotions and lock my feelings down, just hoping that I don't fuck this up. Alexi leads while Vor and Krill walk either side of her, leaving me to take up the rear. As we exit the corridor and move toward the cage, the crowd screams. They are demanding her death. It's so packed in here that we literally have to push our way through and even with the four of us blocking, some fuckers manage to land a hit on her. I wrap my arm around her waist and keep her flush against my chest, Krill and Vor push in closer wrapping an arm each around me and using their own bodies as a shield for her.

We make it to the cage door and I drop my hold on her, keeping my gaze on her back as Vor, Krill and I stake a step back. I dart my gaze around looking for Alexi but can't spot him. That has my hackles raising. I open my mouth to alert Krill but Anya spins away from the cage door and stalks toward me. She grips my face, pulls me down to her and smashes her lips against mine. Before I can even compre-hend what the hell is happening or kiss her back, she is gone and marching through the cage door. I look around the ring and can't find her opponent anywhere. Last night he was already in there waiting for her.

"Something isn't right," Vor shouts over the noise of the crowd. I look to him then Krill and see both of them look worried.

"Where is Alexi?" I ask. Both of them shake their heads as they look around the crowded pub. I do the same and that's when I spot them in the back. Three of them stand there with black hoods over their head, they can shield their faces but I could spot my brothers anywhere. Relief washes over me, it worked. They heard me through the bug asking them to help. It was the only way I could contact them. Once I found out about the fight, I took a calculated risk and went back to Vlad's office to ask my brothers to help me save Anya. I search around for Vin but can't spot him, which means he is on the roof with a bird's eye view and a sniper rifle ready to strike down anyone. My attention is drawn back to the cage when the referee begins to speak. I can't understand a word he is saying because he is talking too fast and I'm not that good at Russian.

"We have a surprise guest fighter tonight." I keep my face blank and stand up straighter as Krill begins to relay to me what the ref is saying. They know I'm not Russian! "He hasn't been home in years. He was a crowd favorite and it's about time he came home to help run things." Anya looks behind her and outside the cage I can see the crowd parting for whoever it is. Unlike Anya, they don't boo or throw things, they cheer for this bastard. "A family feud will be settled tonight–" Krill's words fall on deaf ears as the crowd parts and Anya's opponent becomes visible to me, my body stiffens and my blood turns to ice inside me. I fucking knew it.

Hasn't been home in years.

Help run things.

Family.

The words play on a loop inside my mind as I watch my brothers most trusted man climb into the ring with a smile on his face.

Chapter Ten

Anya

The moment I see him enter the ring, I cut my gaze to Gage. His eyes are wide with shock, as he flicks his gaze to me and that's when guilt sets in, the look of betrayal on his face stings. I may feel guilty but it's not like I know him or even really trust him in order for me to tell him we had a sleeper inside his brother's network for years. Alek was the only person Vlad was ever able to get close enough to the Murdoch's. The fact that he was brought into the inner circle was something no one saw coming. Alek is the reason Vlad has been able to stay one step ahead this whole time since the previous Don, Tony, was murdered by the hands of his own son.

"Choroso byt doma, dvoyurodny bratt." (*It's good to be home, cousin.*) The shouts of the crowd become white noise as I stand here and stare at my cousin. I haven't seen him in years. He's changed so much. Gone is the soft looking boy I grew up with, in his place is a man hardened by this life and the tolls it takes on them. "Mne priyatno govorit' na moyem rodnom yazyke." (*It feels good to speak in my mother tongue.*)

"Why are you here?" I ask. A cruel smile stretches across his face as he leans in to whisper in my ear and I fight the shiver that wants to break free at his close proximity.

"Because you have been naughty and brought the enemy into our home." I stumble back a step and shake my head, denying his claim. His eyes narrow as he slowly turns his head to look toward the gate, I follow his line of sight and freeze. He stares directly at Gage, panic rises inside me.

"Where's my father?" I snap. Alek lazily turns to face me not caring that the crowd is demanding we fight.

"Away, I'm here to take care of the mess you have made so my dear uncle doesn't need to worry." Bile rises in my throat and I quickly swallow it back down. I need to clear my mind and block everything out in order to fight. I know I don't stand a chance against Alek, he has always been good at everything he does. I won't go down without a fight. I will give him everything I have and not stop until my dying breath.

"We gonna keep talking or we gonna do this?" I growl. He cuts his gaze back to me before letting it trail up and down my body, a look of disgust marring his face. I fight the shiver that wants to break free as his assessing gaze fills me with disgust.

"I'm going to enjoy this after knowing you let the bastard between your legs." His cold harsh words have me fighting not to flinch away. I need to remember that he isn't the person I once knew. Years away have changed him and made him into a monster just like both our fathers. There's no warning when he makes his move. He moves so fast I don't see it coming until I'm stumbling to the side and pain reverberates through my cheek. I try to right myself and get my feet under me, but I'm struck by a fist to the other side of my face. My vision turns hazy and I stumble backward until my back smacks against the cage, forcing the breath from me. I manage to get my guard up before he can land another blow. I grunt through the force of his hits and weather the pain, but when he alternates from punching to kicking me in the stomach, I double over. On my hands and knees, I retch and can't stop myself from gagging.

I cry out when he grips my hair and yanks so hard, I swear I feel strands being torn from the roots. An anguished shout draws my attention. I flick my eyes to the left and see Gage gripping the gate trying to yank it open, his eyes wide and filled with panic. It shouldn't bring me comfort knowing that he cares but it does. At least someone will care when I die. Alek grips my chin and tightens his hold on my hair. I close my eyes and wait, thankful he isn't drawing this out and inflicting more pain on me when he and I both know he could have, no one would have stopped him. I tense as his grip tightens and try to prepare for what is about to happen, but the truth is, how do you prepare to die? There is nothing you can do, no matter what you try and tell yourself or even if you think you are ready. When the moment comes, you aren't. All the things I wish I had the chance to do flash before my eyes. The yearning of wanting to be free and find love for myself hits me in the chest, and I feel the lone tear trail down my cheek.

"Fuck!" Alek roars behind me and then his grip on me is gone. At the sound of panicked screams and the unmistakable sound of gun fire rings out around me, I snap my eyes open. Chaos ensues, the screams of the patrons that came here tonight to watch me die, fight and push their way toward the exit. All they are doing is causing a fucking stampede. My attention is pulled to the gate when I hear my name being shouted. I see Gage, Krill and Vor trying to break it open. I pull my gaze from them to peer over my shoulder and gasp when I see Alek on his back with a pool of blood around him. That has me snapping out of my daze and I push to my feet and stagger, my head swims and I begin to feel dizzy. I close my eyes hoping it will help clear the dizziness from my head. The screams of the crowd and the piercing sound of gunshots do nothing to help ease the pounding in my head.

"Find the fucking key!" I hear Gage shout. I blink my eyes open to see Vor and Krill darting on either side of the cage to go in search of the guard with the key. Gage beckons me over with a look. I stumble the first couple of steps, until I manage to right myself before I fall flat on my ass. His eyes narrow as one side of his lip pulls back in a sneer. When I finally reach him, I collapse against the cage breathing raggedly. I can feel the light sheen of sweat on my forehead, guessing two nights in a row of getting the shit beaten out of me has finally taken a toll. My legs give out and I slide down the side of the cage until my ass meets the ground. Gage crouches down and grips the cage, I can see a war of emotions in his eyes.

Anguish.

Regret.

Pain.

Awe.

...longing.

"Is he dead?" My voice sounds strained to my own ears. It's a stupid question but I need to focus on something else aside from the pain radiating throughout my body. I feel the tears building at the back of my eyes and will them away, I'm not an emotional person.

"Yeah, Ubiytsa (*killer*), he is."

I nod, accepting his answer and not for a second feeling any type of remorse for my cousin, who was willing to end my life all because Vlad ordered it. I shake my head before leaning it back against the fence and closing my eyes, exhaustion weighing heavily on me. I know I should fight it and try harder to get out of here before Vlad or the Crows show up but I just don't have it in me to fight anymore. I'm so fucking tired of waking up each day to fight. If it's not in the ring then it's at the club or at the shipping company I oversee for Vlad. I find it comical that aside from the skin trade his most successful business is the drugs. That is one fucking thing even he can't deny I am good at. Because of me, Vlad has been able to export cocaine worldwide and never be caught. It's such a fucking simple task and yet no one has ever thought to use the methods I do. Cocaine in its liquid form mixed into plexiglass, once hardened you can't detect any traces of it, but once they are melted down, the components naturally separate without ever mixing. That means, you have ninety-six percent pure cocaine.

I feel my consciousness slipping away. The sound of the chain rattling tells me someone is trying to get in to kill or rescue me. I fight with everything inside me to open my eyes and push myself to my feet. My vision swims for a second before it finally clears, flinching when another round of shots rings out. Hands grip my arms and I try to pull free until I see its Krill. He curses beneath his breath and scoops me up into his arms before dashing out of the cage. Jostling in his arms makes me feel queasy, so I close my eyes and try to block out everything happening around me.

Chapter Eleven

I watch Krill race from the cage with Anya tucked against his chest. I grit my teeth and pull my gaze from her as I turn to chase after my brothers. They race through some back door I didn't even notice and keep running through the streets. People are scattered everywhere running for their lives. All hell broke loose when Vin shot Mav. Fuck, I knew he was a snitch bitch but I had no fucking idea that he was a Russian playing spy in my brother's organization. Bishop and King trusted him. Me and Knight knew he was hiding something and were proven right when the fucker went missing.

"The car's stashed just up there!" King shouts. I can't see where he is pointing but keep following them. I have no choice, my cover is blown whether I want to believe it or not. There is no way that they don't pin this on me. A beaten-up Honda Civic comes into view. Bishop races to the driver side while the rest of us pile into the back and front seat. Bishop rams the key in the ignition before planting his foot and getting us the hell out of dodge.

"Take your next left and go to the end, Vin will be waiting there." Knight answered my unasked question without even knowing it, Bishop does as instructed and sure enough as we near the end of the road, Vin steps out of the shadows. I scoot over and ride bitch. He just manages to get inside before Bishop is planting his foot again. Vin manages to yank the door closed and shoots Bishop's a glare, not that he can see it.

"You got the kill shot, right?" Bishop demands, when Vin hesitates, unease creeps up my spine. I turn to look over at him. The angry glint in his eyes makes me believe he didn't get the kill shot.

"If he gets help within an hour he'll live," Vin grits out, clearly pissed at himself for missing the head shot. King turns to peer around his chair with an irritated look in his eyes.

"How the fuck did you miss? Aren't you supposed to be the *Bloodhound*?" King's mockery of Vin's skillset clearly pisses the big fucker off, so before they can get into, I cut in.

"What happened? You should have taken him out before he hit her!" I can hear the bite in my own voice, but I keep my face blank so the others don't pick up on my anger.

Vin turns to face me as he answers. "Mav wasn't on his own, I had the shot lined up and then I was attacked on the fucking roof." I scan his face and that's when I see the small tear on the shoulder of his shirt, a slight discoloration on his cheek which will no doubt turn into a bruise. Fuck. If he wasn't on his own then that means—

"It was a setup." Knight takes the words right out of my mouth. If Vin was ambushed on the roof then that means Mav set this whole thing up to draw us out. How the fuck did he know we were in Russia?

"We need to regroup and come up with a new plan. Gage's cover is blown so we need a new way in." I clench my fists, pissed off that what Bishop says is true. This was my shot at proving to them that I was worthy enough to be seen as an equal and I fucking blew it because of *her*.

We pull up to an abandoned looking building, the place looks like it has been raided and burnt out. I follow the others out of the car expecting to enter the windowless building, when they veer right to head around the back, I don't question it. I've never seen where they have been staying as we haven't even spoken since the day I landed here weeks ago. I'll admit, I had doubted that they would show tonight. I didn't think I meant enough to them to even bother to help me but I was wrong. Them showing up tonight showed me that they do care, they may never say it but they took a huge risk coming to that fight outnumbered and outmanned.

King stops at the back of the building in front of a cellar door, he bends and lifts it open before heading down. Vin motions for the rest of us to follow, I trail after Knight and make sure to take care as I descend the stairs. It's dark as shit and it's only when we reach the bottom that a light flickers on. I look around the confined space surprised as hell. They have stretchers set up for their makeshift beds, a shelf in the corner which houses canned food and a couple desks in the corner with computers. They have been living like this for weeks and I had no fucking idea. This has to be hard for Bishop. He's the head of the mafia in New York and yet here he is living like a common homeless man.

"You thought your hostel was bad, huh?" King's attempt at humor doesn't hit its mark, all I feel is guilt for them living like this. I turn to Bishop surprised to see his gaze is already on me. I open my mouth but he beats me to it.

"Don't fucking look at me like that, I do whatever I have to ensure my family remains safe and on top." He doesn't wait for a response as he brushes past me to head through a doorway I didn't notice earlier. I'm shaken from my stupor when Vin claps a hand on my shoulder. I can see from the hard set of his eyes that he is pissed with himself for missing the kill shot. Vin never misses and technically he didn't, he still saved Anya.

Three days later...

This fucking cellar is too small for the five of us!

There is nowhere to hide or even get a minute to yourself, I am going to wind up hitting one of them soon. Bishop barks orders like there is no tomorrow. King paces every square inch of this place. Knight grunts and types continuously on the computer next to Vin who fucking whistles nonstop! I grip my hair and tug on the strands. Being around them all the time back home was fine because we had enough space in the house to escape each other, or I could just go back to my place above the gym!

"Find a fucking way in, this shit needs to be polished, Knight," Bishop barks. He is a tyrant and hates the fact he has to rely on his kid brother to do it for him. Bishop needs control, thrives on it even, when he doesn't have it he acts like he is now, being a dick.

"You want to swap seats and hack the fucking Russian governments files?" Knight snaps, clearly fed up with Bishop and all his demands. Can't blame him. "It's not going to take five fucking minutes, asshole. You breathing down my neck doesn't fucking help!"

"The quicker you find a way in, the quicker we use it against them and get the fuck out of here!" Bishop's words seem to strike something in Knight, his eyes narrow and his upper lip twitches.

"I'm the one missing out on seeing my fucking kids growing inside my girl so don't fucking stand there and tell me how fast to move." Knight's anger can be seen in his face and the way his body is poised and ready to fight. For a moment I forgot all about Koby being pregnant. This whole situation must be fucking hard for him, on top of everything else he was just able to finalize Koby's divorce to Vlad yesterday. He should be ecstatic but he isn't as he can't even call her to tell her the good news.

"Everyone needs to take a break," I cut in, trying to defuse the situation before these two start throwing hands. The last thing we need in this small as fuck space is Bishop and Knight fighting. Four sets of eyes turn to me, each of them stares at me like I have lost my freaking mind. I throw my hands up and push on. "We need a way in, yes, but we also need to think better about this."

"How so?" Vin asks. I run a hand through my hair as I answer them.

"You have been watching the video feeds for three days. Anya hasn't returned to any of Vlad's clubs, hotels, houses or even her own dump of an apartment." Bishop and King eye me skeptically, before they can butt in I carry on. "Anya

Volkov is our way in." Bishop's eyes crinkle at the corners, his eyes blazing with mistrust. He has been on edge and questioning everything since seeing Mav in the ring with Anya. Bishop trusted him and if the fucker did survive, he is going to wish he didn't when Bish gets his hands on him.

"And why would you think that?" B grits out.

"Because the girl hates her father. In my time with them I picked up on the fact she controls his assets. If you want information about bringing Vlad and Ivan down, Anya is the way to do it."

King scoffs as he says, "Let me guess, you can get her onside?"

I nod. "Damn fucking right I can. That girl wants me and I am going to use that against her to take down her whole fucking family." I hate that a pang of guilt that hits me in the chest as I say that out loud. Truth is, Anya isn't the only one who caught feelings in a short fucking time. I also have to come clean to my brothers and tell them that Anya knows where Rook is and that he is alive.

Chapter Twelve

Anya

It's been four days since the fight against Alek. I'm able to move easier now but the bruises that mar my body and face make it look worse than what it is. I know Vlad is going to be hunting for me, I don't have my phone or anything on me. They were left behind when we fled. Krill, Vor and I have been holed up in a remote cabin up in the mountains as protocol dictates that if there is a hit on a high-ranking member, we are to retreat to one of the many safe houses and lay low until we are called back. Krill says Vlad and Ivan haven't called once so that means they haven't found Gage. I won't lie, that knowledge has me breathing easier.

I don't know how he is avoiding them in their own territory, but what that tells me is Gage isn't in Russia alone, he has help with him. That thought has me feeling less tense knowing that he has people watching his back. I knew Gage wasn't Russian from the first moment I saw him come in for intake. The fake accent was a dead giveaway. I put Vor and Alexi on and made them bunk in the hostel to keep an eye on him. Vlad has no idea I did that but he doesn't pay attention to me anyway. The sound of Krill's phone ringing snaps me from my thoughts. He answers on the second ring, grunts, then moves toward me in the small living room, holding the phone out.

I don't miss the sad look he shoots me when I take the phone and place it against my ear. "Da," I answer.

"You stupid fucking bitch!" I flinch at the angry voice, the fact he is speaking in English tells me he isn't alone and doesn't want whoever he is with him to understand what he is saying. "You fucking ruined everything. Your uncle is going to fucking flay you for this." I cringe, I forgot for one blissful second that Alek is dead.

"I had nothing to do with that–" I try to defend but he cuts me off.

"You have started a war with the Americans that they can never win, you helped that suka (*bitch*)."

"I didn't help anybody, I swear, Otets (*father*). I would never betray the family or the Bratva like that." Vlad goes silent for a moment, giving me time to catch my breath and try to think of a way out of this. He thinks I am loyal to him because we share blood. I'm only loyal and stick around because I am terrified of what will happen to me if I left. I regret not running with Dimitri and Koby but I knew if I did, he wouldn't stop hunting. With me here, I had a chance to distract him and keep him off her trail. The three of us didn't pay the price though. Ivan had another son, Dante, he wasn't like the others. He was good, kind, soft and loving. Vlad blamed Dante for Koby and Dimitri escaping. I tried to offer my life for his but Vlad wasn't having that. The moment he pulled that trigger and killed my best friend, I knew I would do whatever I had to take him down.

"You draw this American out. You use whatever means you have, if it means he fucks your ruined cunt then you let him. I want his fucking head, Anya. Don't return until you have done it. Fail me and your end will be worse than your cousins."

Fear rushes through me but I manage to speak even if it sounds robotic to my own ears. "Da, Pahkan."

———

Two days later....

Six days since the fight and still we remain banished. Vor went into town yesterday and gathered some supplies. He even managed to pick up a couple laptops and a printer so we are able to work from here while still trying to come up with a plan. Krill tells me that Vlad has men hunting for Gage around the clock. It is only a matter of time before he is found, I need to get to him first. If I fail, I have no doubt Vlad will give in and hand me over to Ivan as punishment for failing him. The thing is, I would slit my own throat before letting that *suka* ever touch me again!

"Did you know?" I lift my gaze from my laptop and peer over at Krill, who is sitting on the other end of the sofa by me. He and Vor look like they haven't slept in days. I can see that this mission is weighing on them and both of them know, if I fail, so do they and they will pay with their lives.

"Know what?" I ask.

"That the Bloodhound was at the fight and he is the one who shot Alek?" My eyes widen in surprise.

"He's here, in Russia? Why?" Krill shakes his head before returning his attention back to his laptop. He hits a few keys then turns it toward me. Right there on the screen is the face of the Bloodhound racing down the street near where the fight was held.

"He's either here with the American's or they sent him to take out Alek because they discovered he was one of us." I can't explain it but I just know he is here with Gage which means, so are his brothers. Dread pools inside me. I lied to him. I used him and now when he comes for me to get the intel he needs to find his brother, he'll know I've lied.

I open my mouth to ask Krill what happened to Alexi but his phone rings, cutting me off. Vor chooses that moment to walk in and drop into the single seater across from us, kicking up his feet to rest on the small table between us.

"Da?" Krill snaps once he answers the call and holds the phone against his ear. He tenses for a split second before turning to me, this time when he holds the phone it isn't a look of pity on his face. He looks confused, angry, betrayed and something else I can't quite put my finger on. He hands the phone to me and I hesitantly reach for it, I know whoever is on the phone isn't my father or uncle. I tentatively place the phone against my ear while still holding Krill's gaze as I answer.

"Da?" A husky laugh that fills my ear has my eyes widening.

"No call, no text, just radio silence after I give you the best orgasm of your life?" I feel the heat creeping up the back of my neck. Gritting my teeth, I try to fight the flush from finding its way to my cheeks.

"What do you want?" I'm proud that my voice doesn't tremble. The truth is, I'm relieved he's alive and okay. The problem though, I need to push the feelings I have toward him out of my head and remember who I am and what I have to do.

"Skipping the foreplay I see." I pinch the bridge of my nose and take a calming breath. Gage is acting like a fool and it is working on my nerves.

"Get to the point of this call before I hang up." Him calling me on Krill's phone is a huge risk. I need to keep the bored expression on my face so neither of the two men watching me see the effect hearing his voice has on me.

"Fine. I know where you are and I want a face-to-face meet." Gone is his carefree tone, only to be replaced by a stern *don't fuck with me* tone. I dart my gaze toward the windows, thinking I will be able to catch a glimpse of him. It's stupid, I know he would be better at hiding and I would only be able to see him if he wanted me to see him.

"That can't happen–" He cuts me off before I can finish.

"It can and it will. You owe me and I'm here to collect. Make an excuse or whatever it is you need to tell your guards. You have forty minutes." The line goes dead before I can even argue with him. I hand the phone back to Krill then drop my gaze to my lap. I sit here for a minute silently gathering my thoughts and thinking of what I need to say–how I have to tell them that their enemy is coming here and not get shot in the head. These two men are loyal to the Bratva. What I am about to tell them is going to either cost me my life, or to be turned over to Vlad and wish that they had just killed me. I shift nervously on the couch. I know Krill isn't packing heat but I'm not sure about Vor. If need be, I could easily outrun them to the front door and try to lose them in the woods if this goes sideways.

"The American's are coming–"

Vor cuts me off before I can even finish speaking.

"You need to listen to what we have to say." The serious look on his face and the firmness of his tone has me sitting about straighter. "Let us tell you a story about the *Crows*."

Chapter Thirteen

The fact that we are all in one car isn't exactly ideal, the tension rolling off Bishop is making us all uneasy. Luka sent through an encrypted email alerting him to the fact that we have had some blow backs with taking over the territories. We knew it would happen but none of us expected to be out of the country when it did. Luka assures him that he has it handled and is dealing with it but Bishop being the control freak that he is hates not being there to ensure everything is running smoothly. We have a plan in place now. Knight managed to send through an email to Tony Bennett that can't be traced. Bish may hate asking his future father-in-law for help but with the rebellion happening back home, we don't have near enough men to go after the Bratva without Tony.

"Pull over here," Bishop instructs King. He pulls the car off the side of the road half a mile away from the cabin Anya is in. We're going in blind here and none of us like it, but this is where Vin's skill set comes in handy. He will lead the hunt, with King and Knight going in second. Then Bishop and I will come in last. Each of us has our own strengths and now isn't the time for us to measure dicks and get uptight about it. Vin goes to the trunk of the car with the rest of us following after him. All of us reach in and grab vests, guns, knives and whatever else we can get our hands on. My cock may betray me where Anya is concerned but my head won't. I know she means well but at the end of the day, she is still Vlad's daughter which means I can't trust her.

"Here." I turn to Vin and eye the earpiece in his hand. I look to my brothers to see the three of them placing one in their ears. "I'll loop you all in once I'm positioned and deem that it's clear." I nod, take the ear bud and place it in my ear. Vin takes off through the woods without another word, leaving the four of us here in awkward silence.

"Did you fuck her?" Well, the awkward silence didn't last long enough. I turn to Bishop, his eyes search for an answer without me having to speak. Tension is always present when he and I are together, he can't let go of the fact that I slept with Kiara. I feel like shit about it but the truth is, she needed me and I would do it again because I love her. I thought she and I would end up together. But the first time I saw her and Bishop together, I knew she would never be mine because she was always his. It hurt for a long time seeing them together, now though, all I feel is happiness for them both. Bishop has brought Kiara back to life and she has given my brother something to fight for. He always fought for our family but now, he fights twice as hard because of her.

"Would it make you feel better if I say yes?" I deadpan, keeping a serious look on my face. Bishop's eye narrow, he takes a step forward but Knight snakes an arm out stopping his movement.

"Don't start this shit, we have bigger problems to deal with instead of your hurt ego." I bite down on my bottom lip to stop my smile from breaking free at Knight's words. Not one to be deterred though, Bishop asks again.

"Are you fucking the Russian?" I hold his gaze as I answer.

"No, I'm not." His shoulders relax slightly. King steps up beside Bishop and runs his gaze over me. He is calculating and it makes me feel uneasy, almost like he can see through my half-truth.

"You're not fucking her but you are doing *something* with her." There it is, trust King to be the one to put it together. I debate lying but decide to just go with the truth, they are going to figure it out when they're in the same room with me and her. The sexual tension between me and Anya is thick and you would have to be blind not to feel it.

"Yeah, I am." Bish opens his mouth to tear me a new one but I quickly push on. "I needed to gain her trust and I did. I got into her father's office and bugged it. I even managed to lay a bug in the locker room and slip one in Alexi's pocket before the fight." King and Bishop both look surprised by this news. Knight, on the other hand, just nods his head in respect.

"She is the enemy, don't forget that," is all Bishop says as he and King turn away to talk, fuck knows what about and honestly, I don't give a shit. I move toward the front of the car away from the others and sit down on the hood while we wait for Vin. My peace is short lived when Knight stands in front of me. I sigh as I run a hand down my face, I'm so not in the mood to fight with him.

"You never gave up on helping me track Rook." His words crush me, guilt has been eating at me daily for not coming clean and telling them about the picture Anya gave me. I know I should but if there is a chance she keeps to her word and kills him if I snitch, I'll just have to find a way to deal with the guilt until I get him back. "For that, I'll make sure that no harm comes to that girl if she means anything to you." I search his gaze and find nothing but the truth, he would protect her for me and not his baby mama. In Knight speak, this is his way of showing me that we are good and that alone has a sense of pride washing over me.

"She means nothing to me," I answer. He quirks a single brow at me and shakes his head.

"Your mouth says one thing but your eyes say another. You may not want to admit it but you like this girl and she is weaving her way under your skin." I grit my teeth, annoyed that he isn't wrong about me caring for Anya. For some unknown fucking reason, I do care about what happens to her. I see my own fucking redemption in her eyes. I hate that I am going to have to use her like she has been used by her father her whole life. The sound of Vin's voice in my ear has me standing straight and ready to get this shit done.

"In position, everything is clear, three in the house and no guards outside." King and Knight both set out ahead of us, they will each take a separate route and make sure there isn't someone that Vin missed. Minutes tick by and I begin to get anxious as Bish and I wait for word that the coast is clear. Bishop and I are both leaning against the side of the car, the tension between the both of us nauseating. I hate it but I can't change the past and fix what I broke.

"I'm sorry," I blurt. I feel him shift beside me. The pressure of his gaze boring into the side of my head makes me wish I never spoke but I man up and push on, while keeping my gaze focused ahead. "I never should have done what I did with Kiara." The growl that sounds from deep within his chest alerts me to the fact I need to make my point fast or we are going to be throwing hands in seconds. "I didn't know what she was to you then–"

"You knew exactly who the fuck she was to me, I told you to watch out for her!" I finally turn to face him. Anger shines in his eyes but for a split second I see remorse before he quickly masks it.

"Exactly! You told me to watch out for her, Bishop. You never told me she actually meant *something* to you. Yes, I knew about the marriage but I didn't know you loved her." He eyes me skeptically for a second before he answers.

"Would it have changed anything?" A whoosh of air escapes me as I nod.

"It would have changed everything! I would never have... done it or even let her fight. Me teaching her to fight was my way of helping her, you didn't see her the night I found her, Bishop. She was fucking terrified, her own shadow scared her for fuck's sake. She needed to focus on something other than her past. I promised to teach her to fight if she kept her grades up at school."

"Why didn't you tell her that the scholarship was from me?" A sad smile crosses my face.

"Because she thought she was so special that a school reached out to her and wanted her to join them. For the first time she was truly happy. She saw it as her way out. I couldn't shatter that for her." I hate myself for lying to her. Kiara–shit, even Ally and Koby are like sisters to me. Bishop sighs and runs a hand through his hair, some of the tension drains from his body which allows me to relax slightly.

"You teaching her to fight was a... good thing." A cocky smile spreads across my face causing him to groan. "I want to blame you for sleeping with her but the truth is... it's my fault because I should have been man enough to claim my girl a long time ago." His words shock me to my core. "What you did for her, I can never repay you for that. You saved her when I didn't know she needed saving. I... I am indebted to you, Gage. As a way to try and repay that debt you should know, I had Luka file the paperwork to have your name changed legally from Matthews to *Murdoch*." My mouth drops open in shock, I always wanted to be a Murdoch. Not because of that cunt Tony, but because I wanted to share the same last name as my siblings. I just never thought they–Bishop really would ever accept me enough to allow this.

"W-why?" He pulls his gaze from me and stares ahead with a blank look on his face.

"You've always been a Murdoch, Gage. It was just a matter of time before you became one in name."

"But I haven't taken the Bratva down!" He lulls his head to the side and gives me an *are you stupid* look.

"It was never about that. The fact that you would even risk your life just to infiltrate them to help us when we have done nothing for you, proves you are one of us." I'm man enough to admit that his words have me choked up. "I know you're close to all the girls. I doubt I will ever be okay with you spending so much time with *my* girl but... I trust you." Hearing that Bishop trusts me is like hearing your father tell you he is proud of you for the first time in your life. Before we can continue our conversation, King and Knight both give us the all clear to approach.

Ready or not here I come, baby.

Chapter Fourteen

Anya

Trepidation thrums through me, my mind is reeling from what Vor and Krill have just told me. I don't know what I am supposed to do or how to even process what I have just learned. On top of all of that, Gage will be here shortly and I don't think I can deal with any more information today or I will fucking explode. My whole world as I knew it has been flipped upside down. If what I have learned is true, then there is no way I can ever return to my old life. I've been outed and if my father or uncle find out, my punishment will be worse than ever before. I know for a fact Ivan would enjoy doling out my punishment. Vlad has allowed him to *play* with me before but never allowed it to get too far. Ivan is worse than Vlad, he enjoys carving you up and relishes in the screams of agony you emit.

"You have a choice," the sound of Vor's voice pulls me from my thoughts. "Help us and we can help you. We will honor your terms." I eye each of them, seeing them in a new light and berating myself for not being able to see it sooner.

"How can I trust your word?" I hedge. Before Vor can answer me, Krill jumps to his feet dashing to the kitchen and grabs his gun off the counter. *Show time.* Vor moves to the nearest window, I lift the couch cushion I was just sitting on and grab my gun I stashed under there. I silently move toward the window near the front door and peel the curtain back just enough so I can peek out of it. My breath lodges in my throat. Either they are the stupidest mobsters in history or they have the whole place surrounded and will have us put down within a second of stepping foot outside. Gage stands there next to a man that I recognize well, Bishop Murdoch, Don to the Murdoch mafia and head of the New York crime family. Unlike Gage, Bishop looks hardened by this life. His eyes are dark and calculating, his posture is ridged, he can wear all the thousand dollar suits he likes but it will never hide the fact there is a killer beneath those clothes.

Gage looks relaxed, at ease even. He doesn't dart his gaze around or fidget, just stands there with his hands shoved into his jean's pockets. I drink him in. He wears a navy hoodie with the hood pulled up—his man bun should have been the first thing to give him away when he came to Russia. The only reason he was given a chance to prospect for us is because he came recommended by Marco Murelo, but upon meeting Gage, I knew who he was straight away. His ruggish bad boy looks didn't sway me but his eyes, they did the trick. His green eyes burn with an intensity that has you thinking he can see right into your soul. I don't know what it was but the longer I stared into his eyes, the more I began to hope that he would be the one to set me free.

"I know you're watching me, killer." I tense, his eyes haven't moved at all but I get the sense he knows exactly where I am. A shiver races down my spine when he lazily turns his head and stares right at me–or the window—who fucking knows, but it causes me to drop the curtain and jump back a step. His boisterous laughter grates on my nerves. "Come on, killer, don't be shy now. I mean, would you like me to jog your memory of a time you weren't too shy to scream my name?" I cringe and quickly cut my gaze to Krill, shaking my head, trying to deny Gage's claim. Krill just quirks a brow as if mocking me. Yeah, he knows I'm full of shit. I push past Krill and head straight for the front door needing to get out there and cut Gage off, the fucker is retelling the story of how he ate me out!

I throw the door open and glare right at him. I'm seething when the bastard smiles wide. "You have the biggest fucking mouth!" I snarl, which only serves to make him laugh. I cut a glance to Bishop who seems fine with Gage taking the lead on this situation. Gage's laughter dies when Krill and Vor step out of the cabin and flank me on either side. Before they can move a single muscle, two red lasers are pointed to each of their chests. I grind my teeth in anger as I glare out at the woods in front of me.

"Awww, baby, you didn't really think we would come alone, did you?" I turn my attention back to Gage and scowl at him.

"Quit your shit. I liked you better when you were silently brooding in the corner," I deadpan.

"Really? And here I was thinking you liked me better on my knees eating your pussy." I feel heat in my cheeks and bite down on my tongue. I don't blush, *ever*! The fact that Gage Matthews was able to draw such a reaction from me isn't a good thing, he's burrowed himself deeper inside me then I thought.

"Why are you here, Gage?" I decide to cut right to it, I don't like standing out here in the open. With two lasers trained on my guys, I'm pretty much a sitting duck. The carefree look he was sporting a second ago vanishes when he turns to his brother who nods subtly. Dread begins to pool inside me, I don't like the way he has just walled off his emotions, his eyes cold and assessing.

"Because you are going to help me–us, take your father down." Vor shifts next to me, in a split-second Bishop has his gun drawn and pointed right at Vor who growls in annoyance.

"You make one move, *one* fucking move and I will end you." The authority in Bishop's voice has even me wanting to obey him. Not wanting to let this get out of hand considering we have no idea how many men they have surrounding us, I cut in before Vor can speak.

"What exactly is it that you want my help with? Vlad has tasked me with bringing you in. I have lost my leverage here, Gage." It pains me to admit that shit out loud, if I'm being honest, I'm also embarrassed to admit my own father doesn't care if I live or die. I know Vlad, if I'm not back within five days I'm as good as dead. He never has to say it or give me a timeframe, I just know how he works.

"You may have but we haven't." That piques my curiosity. "Invite us in and we'll explain more." Tension ripples through me. He must see the uneasy look on my face because he sighs and continues to say. "We're not here to fight, Anya, we're here to put an end to the Bratva. I promised you that I would help you takeover and I intend to try keep my word!" I'm taken back by the angry tone of his voice, he almost seems annoyed that I want to takeover.

<hr>

We are all gathered in the tiny living area. Turns out they only had his two brothers and Vincent Murelo with them. I can't help but stare at Vincent. He is a legend in the underground world. The only way to better explain who he is and what he does is to compare him to *John Wick*.

"Stop fucking staring at him!" The curt tone of Gage's voice pulls my attention to him, his eyes narrowed and his mouth set in a firm line. He's pissed off... why? A condescending snort comes from behind him. King and Knight both stand there trying to hide their smiles. Gage is sitting between Vin and Bishop. The sight of the three of them crammed on the small sofa makes me want to laugh. Krill and I sit in the recliners while Vor stands on my other side.

"I wasn't staring, I was... admiring?" It comes out sounding more like a question. Vin stiffens and Gage glowers.

"Admire all you like." My focus is pulled to King as he speaks. "But, just know that if you touch him or try anything, our sister is fucking crazy and will kill you for touching *her* man." Vin tries to hide his amusement but fails. I glare at the five of them, stupid men always think with their dicks.

"I was admiring him because of his reputation, not because of his looks." The smile drops from Vin's face as I look directly at him. "You may all think I am a whore because I am Bratva, but I would never encroach on another woman's territory." A growl tumbles from Gage.

"No one said you were a fucking whore!" I furrow my brow confused by Gage's outburst.

"And why would you care if they did?" Krill challenges. I tune out his and Gage's conversation when I feel Knight's gaze on me. I've tried to avoid looking at him at all costs. They are identical twins and seeing him will cause all the guilt to come rushing back about what happened to Rook.

"Shut the fuck up!" I flinch back in my seat and it's only due to his outburst that I realize everyone was shouting. Knight moves around the sofa toward me. Vor moves to intercept him but I quickly stand and step around him. Gage is by my side the same second Knight stops in front of me. I feel the others surrounding us but don't dare look away. His haunted gaze searches mine. I make sure to keep my face blank but it falters the second I feel Gage's hand on the small of my back. "Where the fuck is he?" He doesn't shout or even raise his voice, but the venom that laces each of his words makes it seem like he screamed right in my face. Tension pollutes the air. Gage's hand grips the back of my shirt tightly alerting me to the fact he kept his word and hasn't told his brothers.

"I don't know what you are –" Knight cuts me off before I can finish speaking.

"See, I would have believed you except for the fact that you have done everything in your power to avoid looking at me. The moment you did finally give in, I saw it in your eyes, I saw the anguish. Now, I will ask you one more fucking time, you Russian bitch, where the fuck is Rook?" Within a second Gage shoves me behind him and is now standing face to face with his brother.

"Don't fucking speak to her like that." Gage sticking up for me is not what I ever expected but I would be a liar if I said it didn't have me feeling... I don't know how I'm feeling but I've never felt like this before. I have watched him for weeks but we don't even really know each other, yet here he stands, defending me against his own blood.

Chapter Fifteen

Gage

Guilt is gnawing away at me the longer I stand here staring into Knight's eyes. He won't find the answers he seeks in my gaze. I have a fucking good poker face, I learned from an early age that I had to learn to mask my emotions or this world would swallow me whole. I hate that I can't tell them about Rook. I'm fucking pissed that she has put me in a position where I have to lie to my brothers, but if it means getting Rook back alive, I'll do whatever I have to. I plan on giving Anya a time frame before I loop the others in on what I know about Rook.

"I'll speak to her however I see fit. She is lying, Gage, and you know it." The accusation is clear in Knight's tone. I implore him with a look hoping he will understand.

"Trust me, please." He stands there for a long tense moment searching my gaze, after a beat he reluctantly nods and steps back.

"Anything happens to him because of *her*, I'm coming after you, *brother*." He spits the last word like it burns his mouth. I don't blame him though.

"Can we all have a seat and get this chit chat over with? I don't know about you lot but I want to get the fuck out of Russia and get back to my girl." Bishop, Knight and King all agree to what Vin said. Instead of reclaiming my original seat, I choose to claim Anya's recliner. Before she can move away, I grip her hips and pull her onto my lap. The gasp that slips free from her sinful lips has me fighting not to smile. She tries to get free but I tighten my hold.

"You do know I am a trained fighter, right?" At her angry tone a small chuckle slips free.

"You do know I train fighters and fight every week against gangsters, right?" She stills in my hold only to peer over her shoulder and shoot me a scathing look that promises pain.

"Pity none of them brought a gun to a fist fight," she snarls.

"Ouch, you wound me, killer."

"Your mother should have swallowed you!" she snaps before focusing forward and causing my brothers to laugh at her stupid remark. "What is it that you all want from me?" she asks no one in particular. Bishop shifts forward in his seat and rests his forearms on top of his thighs, while eyeing Anya with utter contempt.

"I want names, dates, locations and a time and place of when Vlad and Ivan will be together. I want this shit wrapped up within six weeks." Anya doesn't falter in her reply.

"And what is it that I get out of this?"

"Your father not knowing you are a *rata?*" Bishop sounds like a smug prick.

"You can try. The thing is, my father may hate me but he hates you more. All I need to do is make a single call and all airports and private airfields will be shut down within minutes and you will be stuck here in Russia. There is not a place you would be able to hide without him finding you." Bishop grits his teeth in frustration, I on the other hand lean forward and rest my chin on her shoulder ignoring the shudder that rolls through her.

"You said *him* not *us.*" She cringes in my hold, which has a broad smile stretching across my face. "Lie all you want—you and I both know that you don't want to be fighting in that cage every night." A hurt expression clouds her eyes, I'm not trying to be a dick I'm just stating facts and she knows it. "You have a chance here, killer, to get out from under the tyrant who has ruled your life. Help us and I swear *I* will make sure you come out on top." She quirks a brow mockingly.

"On top, huh?" I roll my eyes at her.

"Smartass," I mutter, which just brings a smile to her face. I don't know what it is about her but somehow, she has managed to get me to care enough to not want to see any harm come to her. She turns to Bishop who is already staring at her like she is a puzzle he can't solve.

"The only way I can get access to the information you need is by being back in the city." I unknowingly tense beneath her, she grips my leg subtly and gives it a squeeze. "I won't be able to make contact. I'll find a way to feed you the information you need but you can never contact me. This won't be easy, Vlad doesn't share this information with anyone except Ivan and believe me, my uncle is fucking loyal to my father."

"Get me the information I need and we'll deal with your father and uncle." Anya nods but Bish isn't buying her compliance as easily. "If it comes down to it, are you willing to kill your own father?"

She doesn't falter. "Within a heartbeat." Bish reclines back in his seat with a look I can't decipher on his face.

"And those two." King nods toward Krill and Vor. "Do you trust them enough to not betray you?"

"Yes," she answers, but the slight tremble in her voice tells me she is full of shit.

"How do you plan to get back in Vlad's good graces?" Knight growls out.

"Uh...I'll...I–"

Vin cuts Anya off. "She plans to use Gage as her way back in." The shudder that rolls through her is the only answer I need. When she doesn't answer straight everyone begins to grow tense. King and Knight break away and have their own private conversation. Bishop and Vin never take their gaze off her, so I do what I need to in order to get this shit sorted and moving along. I fucking hate being here in Russia and want to go home.

"I'm not going to be offered up to your prick of father just so you can–" Krill cuts me off before I can even finish. I shoot the fucker a glare.

"You won't be returning to Vladimir, you will be taken elsewhere and kept safe."

"And where the fuck would that be?" I grit out.

"Who the fuck is this guy?" Bishop snaps, Krill ignores Bishop as he focuses on only me.

"You will be taken to the Crows and kept there until

takeover is complete." My jaw unhinges. I peer out the corner of my eye to see Vin and my brothers with confused looks on their faces. I fill them in on who the Crows are and tell them that they want Vlad out as much as us. From the surprised look on their faces, I can tell they had no idea about them like me.

"If the Crows are causing this much trouble for the Bratva, why have we never heard about them before?" Vin asks. It shocks me when Vor answers and not Krill.

"The Crows are an underground network built up of the people of Russia. Each member has somehow been wronged or had a run in with the Bratva. Taking down Ivan and Vladimir is personal for each and every one of us. We want to see their downfall just as much, if not more, than you. Our people need to be liberated. We have lived under the rule of the Bratva for far too long and I will not allow my–I just won't live another year under their rule." I get exactly what Vor is saying. We all lived under Tony's rule for far too long and were only granted freedom to choose what we wanted from our own lives when Bishop took over the family.

"The both of you are Crows." It's not a question, it's a statement Vin is making. Vor and Krill both nod.

"If you want to end the Bratva and are who you say you are, why the fuck were you being a sleezy fucker to Anya in the locker room?" I grit out. Vor at least has the decency to drop his gaze in shame. Anya perks up at my question and stares at Vor questionably. She shifts on my lap to turn her whole body toward him causing me to grit my teeth, and will my dick to not get hard.

"I had to keep up appearances. From what we have seen, the Bratva men treat women like trash." He lifts his gaze and looks at Anya with shame in his eyes. "I swear to you, I would never have laid a finger on you. I'm disgusted with myself for touching you the way I did." Anya's mouth pops open and her eyes widen as a knowing look takes over her face.

"You're married," she states, causing Vor to stiffen. "You hate the Bratva because one of them hurt your wife." She doesn't give him a chance to answer. "You didn't mean yourself before when you said you wouldn't live another year under their rule, you said *my* first. Which means... Oh my god!" All eyes are on her as she slowly pieces together the puzzle none of us managed to. "You have a child!" Vor's eyes widen to the size of dinner plates. I cut a glance to Krill to see him trying to mask his own shock. Anya looks between the two of them and a gasp slips free. "Holy shit, I can't believe I didn't see it before!"

"See what?" I question. She shifts on my lap again to face me causing me to grind my teeth and not get fucking hard. I'm beginning to fail and can feel my cock hardening beneath her.

"They're brothers." I pull my eyes from her to see both Vor and Krill looking uncomfortable. Fucking hell, she's right.

"Is she right?" King asks. Vor and Krill share a loaded look before Krill finally answers for them.

"Yes. We are brothers but Vor isn't a father." My little killer deflates slightly and pouts. I tighten my hold around her waist and pull her back against me, she doesn't fight it. "Vor met his wife the day we rescued our sister from one of the clubs that Ivan had her working at. It took us over a year to find her." The forlorn look in his eyes and the emotionless tone of his voice tells me this story doesn't have a happy ending. "By the time we found her she had a new born baby. We had her back for three days before she killed herself and left the two of us to care for the baby and four other girls we rescued. It was two weeks after that when we found the Crows. Andreas helped us and in return we pledged ourselves to helping him and his cause to take the Bratva scum down!"

Chapter Sixteen

Anya

At the mention of Andreas, the leader of the Crows, I stiffen in Gage's hold. Krill and Vor may have filled me in earlier about their affiliations with the Crows but I couldn't find it within myself to tell them the truth about what happened that night we fought. I tune out the rest of their conversation as I try to work out in my head what is the best plan of action. I know Ivan will be the hardest to fool. He has been waiting for an opportunity to get me in his fucking red room of pain since I was a child. I've never been thankful of father until he stopped Ivan from taking me in there before I left for boarding school in the states. It wasn't until I returned home that Vlad told me the truth about what Ivan does to girls in there. A shudder rolls through me at the thought of being caught trying to take my father down, there is no doubt in my mind he would be the one to throw me in there himself.

"Penny for your thoughts?" I startle at Gage's whispered words. Conversation carries on around us as I peer over my shoulder at him. He smiles warmly and it stuns me, I don't understand why he is being so... nice to me.

"How are you okay with all of this?" I say low enough only for him to hear.

"I could ask you the same thing. You're the one that is going back into the lion's den so to speak." A whoosh of air escapes me and I deflate slightly.

"This is all I have ever known."

"What do you mean?" Each time Gage asks me something, I feel like he hangs onto every word I say. Like he actually cares what I think and that is new for me.

"I'm used to this. The whole wondering if today is the day Vlad finally delivers the final blow." I say it like it's the most normal thing in the world and I know that is twisted and fucked up but it's the truth.

"I won't let him hurt you, Anya." The conviction in which he says this makes me believe him.

"I have to go back, I need to end this."

"I'll help you however I can. Just remember what you promised me though." I nod, unable to speak past the lump in my throat. When he finds out I have lied to him about his brother, he is either going to kill me or make me wish I was dead.

Gage and the others left a few hours ago after coming up with a plan that they think will work. Gage has agreed to stay with the Crows to make my story believable. Krill and

Vor will stay with me and we will return to the city in three days' time. Vor spoke with Ivan and told him that we were chasing down a lead on Gage's location, taking the three days makes our story more believable.

I push away thoughts of what's to come as I stand under the shower head and rinse the conditioner from my hair. I finish scrubbing myself clean before shutting off the water and hopping out to get dry. I wrap my hair in a towel and wrap the other around my body, which still aches but it's nothing I'm not used to. I don't recall a day where I haven't ached in pain since returning home to my father. Vlad has always taken his anger out on me. When Koby wouldn't submit, I'd get beaten. A deal didn't go his way, I'd cop it in the form of screaming in agony while he punched me until I eventually blacked out from the pain. I pull myself from those dark thoughts and open the bathroom that joins onto my master bedroom. I freeze and barely contain my squeal of surprise at the sight in front of me.

The bedside lamp casts a soft glow over him as Gage sits there at the end of my bed with his gaze focused on me. His arms are hanging loosely between his legs. His hair is out and looks like he has run his fingers through it a million times. God, I want to run my fingers through it and feel the silky strands. His eyes are hooded and dark, his lips wet as if he just ran his tongue along them before I came out. This man has raw sex appeal without even trying. I clench my thighs together to try to dull the ache that is forming at my core. When his gaze rakes over my exposed skin a shiver runs down my spine, anticipation beginning to thrum through my nerves when his eyes meet mine. He bites down on his bottom lip as he slowly climbs to his feet like he isn't in a rush—truth be told, I'm anxious as hell to see what he is going to do next.

He stands there nibbling on his bottom lip as he shoves his hands in his pockets, rocking back on his heels as he lazily runs his eyes up and down my body like he has every right to. My body is heating up from the way he is looking at me, like I am the most gorgeous woman he has ever laid his eyes upon. It is an exhilarating feeling to have someone stare at you like you are... everything.

"I have a problem." The husky tone of his voice has me squirming. If the devilish smirk he sports is anything to go by, then he knows exactly the effect he is having on me right now.

"Oh?" If my squirming didn't give me away, the breathy tone of my voice sure as hell does.

"You see, I came here to talk to you about Mav–Alek, as you so happen to know him by, but now I can't seem to string a coherent thought together with you standing in front of me in *that*." He motions with his hand up down my body. Feeling emboldened by this sudden rush of need coursing through me, I reach up and pull the towel off my head letting my hair spring free. I give it a subtle shake enjoying the way his eyes track my every move. Next, I reach up and grip the knot of the towel wrapped around my body. His eyes blaze. I take one last deep breath before I yank it open and allow it to drop to the floor around my feet. "Fuck!"

I fight the smile that wants to break free, as his teeth pierce his bottom lip and a low groan breaks free when he takes in my nakedness. Because I like to tease, I shoot him a wink as I brush past him heading right for my bag at the foot of the bed. I can feel his gaze on me the whole way and make sure to sway my hips. I don't crouch, instead I bend right over as I dig through my bag. The hiss of air that escapes him has me smiling, he's got a front row seat to my exposed pussy and if he looks close enough, he'll be able to see that I'm wet and ready for the taking. The thought of him taking me from behind and fucking me like a savage has my breath hitching and a pulse building between my thighs. I bet Gage Matthews fucks like a man possessed—

A squeal of surprise comes from me when I feel his hands on my hips. I try to stand up straight and turn, but he shifts one of his hands to the middle of my back and turns me so my torso is resting on the bed. Before I can speak, I feel him drop down behind me and then his tongue is swiping through my slick folds,

"Fuck!" I cry out. Gage isn't deterred. He pulls back, only to part my ass and licks from my pussy all the way to my asshole. I tense for a second until he pushes his tongue inside my forbidden hole, then a shameless moan tumbles from my lips. I've never had someone eat my ass before and if I'm honest, the thought of someone doing that to me has always made me embarrassed. But now, fuck, the feeling of his tongue prodding my ass has me panting and my pussy clenching on nothing but air. A long drawn-out moan pulls from me when he grips the globes of my cheeks hard enough to bruise as he fucks my ass with his tongue. A whimper tumbles from my lips when he pulls back.

"Fuck, your pussy looks so good. I've been dying to taste this cunt again, it's the sweetest pussy I have ever tasted." I don't have a chance to say anything before he buries his face between my legs and tongue fucks my cunt. I widen my legs, giving him better access. My nipples are so hard and sensitive, each time I shift and the scrap against the comforter a ripple of desire courses through me. When he sucks my clit into his mouth, I cry out loud enough for Krill and Vor to have heard me. Gage pulls back and lands a blow to each of my ass cheeks causing me to cry out but not from pain... from pleasure. "Shut the fuck up before Sully and Mulder come in here." I turn my head and glare down at him.

"You stop eating my pussy and I'll make sure they kill you."

A cocky smirk pulls at his luscious lips. "If you don't come in the next five minutes, I may die of blue balls. Now bury your pretty fucking face in the bed so I can eat this fucking pussy until you come on my face and then I'm gonna shove my cock deep inside it so you'll know from now on the only cock you will ever ride until I say otherwise is mine!" His words cause me to gasp from the way in which he says those words... like he means them. If Gage wants me to agree to only fucking him, he better make me see fucking stars and give me the best orgasm of my life.

Chapter Seventeen

The taste of her on my tongue has me wanting to moan, I've never tasted a pussy so fucking sweet. I've never been a guy who likes to eat pussy but since the first time I went down on Anya, I haven't been able to stop thinking about how fucking delicious her pussy tasted and have been keening to taste it again. I suck her clit into my mouth and inhale through my nose, the musky scent assaulting my nasal passage and I moan at the smell of her. Her cries only intensify and it spurs me on. I spin around until the back of my head is now against the bed. I grip her ass and pull her pussy down onto my waiting tongue.

"Hold your tongue out like that, I'm gonna ride your face." The neediness in her voice has my hard cock twitching in my pants, I do as she says and groan when she begins to bounce up and down on my tongue fucking my face just the way she likes. She leans back and grips my hair holding my head at the angle she needs as she grinds against my face, I reach up cup her full tits in my hands before pinching her nipples between my fingers. She throws her head back and moans. "God, just like that. Pinch my fucking nipples and suck my clit so I can come!" Because I'm a gentleman, I let her take control this time, but I plan to take charge as soon as my cock is buried deep inside her tight wet heat.

The grip she has on my hair tightens, her thrusts becoming erratic as her moans grow louder, even though she is trying to be quiet. I release her tits and grip her ass as I pull her right to my mouth and suck her clit, she cries out as she comes all over my face. I don't even give her a second to come down from her high. I shift her and climb to my feet. I rid myself of my shirt then my pants are next to go. The moment my cock springs free a gasp sounds from her. I kick my pants to the side and grip my cock in my hand and hiss. My cock is rock fucking hard to the point of pain. I look to Anya only to find her gaze glued to my cock.

I reach out and grip the back of her neck, hauling her to me. Her startled gaze meets mine. Before either of us can overthink this, I smash my lips to hers. We both moan at the taste. I release my cock and use that hand to cup her ass. I move us backward until the backs of her legs hit the mattress. Stepping back, I shove her onto the bed. Her eyes are wide and filled with need. She beckons me to her the moment she spreads her legs wide and puts her perfect pink pussy on display. This woman is a fucking siren!

"You gonna keep looking at it or fuck it?" I quirk a curious brow, I didn't peg her to be a dirty talker.

"I'm just admiring how perfect it looks before I ruin it."

I hold her gaze so she can see the seriousness in my eyes when I speak my next words. "Make no mistake, killer. I'm going to ruin you for any other man. No one will ever be able to satisfy you, fuck you or make you come like I can." Her mouth parts as she inhales a sharp breath. I prowl toward her like we have all the time in the world. I slowly climb up her body, making sure to lick, bite and suck every part of her exposed skin on my way up to her tits, once there I make sure to suck her right nipple into my mouth as I tweak the other between my fingers.

"Shit!" she cries out as her back arches off the bed, forcing her nipple further into my mouth. I release it with a wet pop and make sure to pay the other side the same amount of attention. By the time I reach her lips she is a writhing mess. I capture her lips in a searing kiss, marking her as mine. Anya Volkov may not know it yet, but I plan to keep her as mine until it's time for us to part ways and go back to our normal lives. She cups my face between her hands, deepening the kiss. I nudge her legs wider with my own without ever breaking our kiss. I'm too fucking turned on and needing to be inside her to even worry about a condom. I pull back resting my elbows either side of her head needing to see her face when I push inside her.

"You okay with this?" I give her one last chance to back out. Truth is, it might just fucking kill me if she tells me to stop. My cock has never been this fucking hard and painful before, the only relief for it is to be balls deep inside her. Her facial features soften as she wraps her legs around my waist and urges me forward with them.

"I want you inside me, *now*." I don't fuck around, slowly pushing inside her and relishing in the hazy look in her eyes and the husky moans that tear from her lips. The second I am fully sheathed inside her we both cry out. I quickly slam my lips against hers to quieten her down. With how loud she was before, I'm surprised the two *X-Files* didn't come charging in. I thrust inside her once and moan into her mouth, her pussy is sucking the fucking life out of my cock causing my balls to tighten already. I break our kiss and lean back, then place each of her legs over my shoulders before pushing forward until her feet are on either side of her head.

"This is gonna be hard and fast, I need to fucking come," I grit out.

"Fuck me hard and make me come all over your cock." Jesus, this girl is killing me!

I do as promised, slamming inside over and over again at a brutal pace. A sheen of sweat has broken out over my forehead from the strain of trying not to come has taken on me. I refuse to come without her no matter how hard it is for me. With a growl I pull out of her, much to my cocks displeasure, and use my left arm to rest against her legs, keeping them where they are while I bury two fingers inside her tight cunt. She cries out at the intrusion but I don't stop. I pump into her at the same pace I was just fucking her. She reaches up for one of the pillows above her and slams it over her mouth—clever girl doesn't want me to stop if she gets too loud.

"Don't come on my fingers, I want your come coating my cock, got it?" Her eyes roll back as she nods, a minute later her pussy begins to clench fingers. My eyes widen and I glare at the little minx as I yank my fingers free, her eyes fly to mine. "I said no coming on my fingers!"

"I-I can't, I mean, I wasn't." I narrow my eyes as I slap her cunt. She cries out in shock. "Gage!" I slap her pussy again, she needs to learn that I fucking call the shots in the bedroom. I tell her when she can come and when she can't.

"Back chat me again and I won't be fucking your pussy." Her face contorts in anger at the audacity that I would dare deny her. "I'll be fucking your ass." Her mouth drops open but I can see it in her eyes, that doesn't terrify her it... excites her. "You like that, don't you?" She turns her head away from me. I'm not having it. I resume my original position between her legs and allow her legs to rest on either side of mine before I grip her chin and force her gaze back to mine. Anger shines in the depths of her gaze which confuses the shit out of me. "Why are you mad?"

"I'm not mad," she spits back.

"Don't lie to me or I'll spank your cunt again." She may look at me like she wants to murder me but her body betrays her, a shiver runs through her and her legs tighten around me. "Now, I'll ask again, do you want me to fuck your ass?" She shakes her head *no* but I can see it in her eyes, she wants to say yes but is too afraid to let her inner kink out.

"I don't want that." I don't even bother to respond before I have her flipped on her stomach before she can even try to stop me. She tries to fight me off but it's futile. I use my body weight to pin her to the bed. I brush her hair out of the way as I capture her lobe between my teeth and bite down gently before sucking it. I release it with a wet pop and make sure that my lips brush the shell of her ear as I speak.

"I don't have lube with me and I'm guessing you don't have any either so, you're going to be a good girl and lay here while I eat your tight little asshole. Only when you are squirming and begging for me to bury my cock in your ass will I stop and allow you to come."

"I never come during sex, only from oral," she sass's back. I chuckle darkly in her ear before biting down harder on her lobe. This time until she cries out.

"You've never been fucked by *me*. I'm going to make you come from fucking your ass, then when we catch our breaths, I'm going to fuck your cunt and you, my little killer, are going to come all over my cock and milk it for everything it is worth." My words have a shiver rolling through her body. I slowly slide down her body until I'm standing at the edge of the bed. I knead her cheeks in my hands and smirk when an unsanctioned moan spills from her. Parting her cheeks I lean down and swipe my tongue over her virgin hole. She tries to shift away but not hard enough, she is trying to pretend she doesn't like her ass being eaten but she's full of shit. To prove my point, I push my tongue inside her ass and push a finger inside her pussy, sure enough it is soaking fucking wet.

"Gage, I... shit... like that." I continue to eat her ass whilst simultaneously fingering her pussy. Within two minutes she is shaking and I can tell she is nearly ready to come. I pull back spit in my hand before covering my cock with my spit. I grip her thighs and pull her to the edge so she is leaning over the bed but standing on her tiptoes. I part her cheeks and allow a dollop of spit to fall from my mouth onto her asshole. She gasps at the feeling. Before it can slide down further, I push forward and use my cock to stop it. I gently push inside her hole and stop when the head of my cock breaches her muscle wall.

"Relax, just breathe through it and relax or it will hurt," I grit out through clenched teeth. A cold sweat has broken out over my body and it is taking everything inside me not to slam inside her ass right now and come!

"I can't do this, pull out and I'll.... suck your cock or something."

"Just breathe, Anya, I promise you you'll love this as much as I will." I wait until she relaxes before pushing in further. She doesn't stop me and I am so fucking thankful. When I'm nearly all the way in she tells me to just slam inside her, so I do. We both cry out but for different reasons. Hers is from pain, mine is from fucking pleasure.

"It hurts!" she whimpers. I reach down and grip her arms hauling her up until her back is flush against my chest. I grip her chin and turn her head so I can capture her lips in a kiss. After a second she melts into me and kisses me back. I cup her cheek and wrap my other arm around her waist as I slowly pull out, then glide back in. She whimpers at first but after the third time she is pushing her ass back into me and moaning into my mouth. I break the kiss and bite down on her shoulder, she tilts her head to the side giving me better access. "Oh God, fuck that feels so good."

I suck on her shoulder and relish in the cry that comes from her, I reach around and slip a finger through her folds and growl my approval when I feel how wet she is—it's slick between her fucking thighs! I begin to circle her clit and she cries out, then kisses me to keep quiet. I feel my balls tightening and know I only have a minute left before I'm coming in her ass! I squeeze her clit between my fingers and fuck her ass at a punishing pace. She reaches up and locks her arms around the back of my neck.

"Yes, like that Gage, make me come while you fuck my tight little ass." Fuck this girl was made for me. A second later she begins to shake in my arms, but before she can scream out, I smash my lips to hers to swallow her screams. After the first aftershock tears through her, I come so fucking hard in her ass that I nearly black out. My knees nearly give out so I do the only thing I can. I turn us so we both fall sideways onto the bed with my cock still buried deep in her ass and the only sounds that can be heard is our heavy breathing.

Chapter Eighteen

Anya

I yawn for the fifth time in twenty minutes since we sat down for breakfast. Krill and Vor shoot my scathing looks but I ignore them. Turns out, they knew Gage was here the whole time and heard everything we were doing last night. They both look as tired as I do, so I'm guessing they didn't get much sleep thanks to Gage keeping me up until after dawn. The man has a stamina like no other. I can't sit or even walk without feeling him. Just thinking about the ways, he fucked me and how he made sure I came every time has desire pooling in my belly. The sound of my bedroom opening pulls me from my thoughts. I look up and fight my smile as I watch Gage saunter into the room, freshly showered and not giving a fuck that Krill and Vor are shooting him death glares. I keep my gaze on my plate as he claims the seat beside me. I gasp when he grips the back of my neck and pulls my face to his. His eyes dare me to defy him but I'm not sure why I would until he kisses me!

He is kissing me right here–out in the open in front of Krill and Vor like it's natural and okay for him to touch me. Him doing this behind closed doors is fine, but he cannot touch me like this in public. I pull back and glare at him. He pins me with a dark look warning me not to argue but he can go to hell.

"What the hell do you think you're doing?" I demand.

"Whatever the fuck I want!" I balk at the audacity of him.

"You cannot do that out here–" Gage cuts me off before I can finish.

"Why the fuck not?"

"Because, we cannot be seen as an item!" How does he not understand this? I'm not trying to be a bitch, I'm trying to keep the both of us alive. If someone were to report this to my father both of us would be dead within the hour.

"So, you'll let me fuck you however I want but won't be seen in public with me?" I furrow my brow confused as hell.

"I don't, Gage–"

"Don't, I get it. You can only touch me and fuck me when no one is around. Sue me for forgetting that you are the heiress and I'm the poor Yank." He abruptly stands from the table and storms out of the room. I stare after him even when he disappears inside my room slamming the door closed behind him. I'm so fucking confused about what just happened, I thought we understood each other but from his reaction, I can tell I was wrong.

"You have no need to hide whatever," I turn to look at Krill and can tell from just looking at him that this conversation is about to be awkward, "it is that is going on between you and Gage around us."

"Oh and I'm just supposed to take your word for that?" I snark. I trusted Krill to some degree before but not Vor. If they think I will trust them at their word, they are mistaken.

"No," Vor's answer stuns me. I expected them to tell me that I could trust them and should spill all my darkest secrets. "Only a fool would trust blindly and from what I have seen, Anya, you are no fool." His words have pride swelling in my chest. Rather than sit here and try to make small talk I go after Gage. As soon as I close the bedroom door behind myself, Gage is on me. He uses his body mass to pin me to the wall, grips the backs of my thighs and hoists me up, then kisses me until I have no other choice but to pull away and drag in lungful after lungful of air.

"Did they buy it?" he asks.

"I think so," I breathe out. Gage's performance earlier was planned. He said we needed to make a show of us sleeping together to see if Krill or Vor would snitch to Ivan or Vlad. It's risky and could cost us both, but Krill and Vor would be fools to betray me when I would out them and their affiliation to the Crows to save my own ass.

"As much as I would love to fuck you senseless." I groan at the thought, Gage is a distraction but of the best kind. "Don't make that noise or I really will fuck you and then neither of us will get any work done before we have to leave." The reminder of having to go back to Vlad is like a bucket of ice water being dumped on me. I wiggle out of Gage's hold and put some much-needed distance between us. After last night it seems like the two of us can't keep our hands off the other. I break the sexual tension in the air by asking a question that I know will kill his sex drive for *now*.

"How did you know Alek was a plant?" He keeps his

face blank of all emotion. I hate that he can do that and keep me in the dark of what he is thinking.

"Simple, he was too good at his job and whenever I would question how he knew things he shouldn't have, he would blow me off and cry to Bishop that I was trying to take his job. I wasn't the only one who thought he was a rat. Knight knew something was up with him as well." I nod my head accepting his answer. Alek was getting sloppy the past six months. I tried to tell Ivan but all that got me was a backhand to the face.

"How did your father manage to get your cousin inside my brother's organization?" I motion for him to take a seat on the bed, he does. I follow and sit on the other side making sure to keep a decent amount of space between us. Gage isn't having any of that. He yanks me forward by my arm and settles me between his legs while he rests back against the wooden headboard. It takes me a few minutes before I finally relax into him, the heat of him pressed against me has me envisioning what his body is capable of and the highs it can bring me. "Focus, killer." I clear my throat to try to disguise the fact I was thinking about him naked, again. He shakes with silent laughter behind me.

"It was simple really. Alek was always a smart kid and could blend in anywhere. But, he didn't need to try hard. When your father was Don, he made a deal with my father for the skin trade. He would allow Alek into his fold so he could learn the ways of the mafia and in return Vlad would conduct business with Tony."

"Wait a fucking second. Tony knew the whole time that Mav was a fucking snitch?" The anger in his tone has me tensing.

"Yes."

"Son of a fucking bitch!" he snarls out. I remain silent

giving him time to process what he has learnt. "Why Mav? He could have sent you and promised–"

"He tried but Bishop was already promised to marry another," I utter quietly. Gage is stiff behind me and I hate that my words have hurt him, but it's the truth. "Vlad offered me first. Tony declined saying that Bishop was promised to wed another and Vlad being Vlad, would not settle for me marrying the spare son as he called King."

"Jesus fucking Christ! These men sell off their fucking kids like they are nothing more than chattel. I'd never do that to my kids." Now it's my turn to tense, Gage notices the shift in me straightaway. "What's wrong?"

I shake my head. "Nothing, what else do you want to know?"

"I want to know why you just clammed up? Is it because I said I wanted kids?"

"I didn't–"

"What did I say about lying to me, Anya?" Now that has me stiffening for a whole other reason. He trails his fingers down my arms causing goose flesh to sprout. "I want to fuck you so badly and I might if you don't distract me right now." I turn and peer over my shoulder, his face is so close so I tempt him by closing the small amount of space between us and kiss him. He moans the moment I push my tongue inside his mouth and grips the back of my neck keeping me in place while he devours my mouth. I'm still sore but I can feel wetness gathering between my thighs. The ache begins to build inside me. A knock sounds at the door causing us to break apart, each of us is breathless and panting.

"You both need to get out here!" Vor's tone is filled with worry which has us both scrambling from the bed and racing out of the room. I follow the sound of the TV with

Gage hot on my heels. Vor and Krill sit in the living room with their attention on the TV. I gasp at what the reporter is saying, this can't be happening!

"What's going on? I can't keep up." I begin to translate what the woman is saying for Gage.

"*Alek Volkov has survived surgery and is being treated in the ICU at this moment. Locals are being warned to stay indoors and not go outside. There is a manhunt for the persons that shot alleged Bratva boss, Vladimir Volkov's nephew. Citizens are being urged to call this number if they have any information regarding this shooting. Local police have five suspects they are trying to find. They are American and hiding in the city.*" Krill shuts the TV off, the four of us stand here silently for a minute, before the shrill sound of a phone ringing has me jumping in fright. Krill pulls his phone from his pocket and answers the call. I know who it is already so I hold my hand out and wait for him to give me the phone. He shoots me a sympathetic look but I ignore it as I put the phone to my ear.

"Da?"

"Find that *suka* (*bitch*) and bring him to me!" Vlad is on a warpath, I need to give him some intel. I know it's not what we discussed but it's the only way to keep his suspicions off me until the time comes to finally shut him down.

"I have a lead on the American, he was spotted the night of the shooting with some of the Crows." I can feel all their eyes on me but don't acknowledge them. I can't, they don't know my father like I do. They think I will walk back in there and get away with surviving the fight, they are so fucking wrong. Vlad is going to beat the shit out of me to prove a point that I will always be less than him. I guess in a way I have been lucky, I have never been raped or molested. I just get beaten and abused. I'm used to it though. Vlad started hitting me when I was four, it went from a slap here and there to punches then to kicks and now he just breaks bones. I hate him so much because of what he took from me. He stole my one chance at happiness all for his own fucking gain!

"Find out where they are hiding him. Be back here before nightfall tomorrow." The line goes dead. My shoulders slump as I hand Krill back his phone and turn to head back to my room. I call over my shoulder,

"We leave tomorrow. Prepare what you need to," is all I say before disappearing inside my room. I need to prepare myself mentally, emotionally and physically for what is coming tomorrow.

Chapter Nineteen

Gage

Anya has holed herself up in her room and hasn't come out for a couple hours. Krill and Vor are making the preparations they need to in order for me to remain with the Crows. I don't relish the idea of walking into unknown territory but we are out of options. If this is the only way to end the fucking Bratva scum, then so be it! I pull the phone Vin gave me from my pocket and walk outside, the crisp afternoon air has me shivering but I can't make this call inside the small cabin. I dial the only number in the phone and wait for them to answer. It's no surprise to me when it's Bishop's voice I hear first.

"What happened?"

"Vlad called her back early, we leave tomorrow to go

back to the city." I hear him curse and relay what I just said to the others.

"Why? What changed?" I take a deep breath and blurt it out.

"Mav is alive and Vlad has us all over the news. The four of you can't leave that bunker. The local army is patrolling the streets and so are the cops. As soon as I can get you safe passage to a private airport, the four of you are to get the fuck out of Russia."

"You don't give the fucking orders around here–"

"I do now, Bishop! I can't fucking fight to stay alive while worrying about the four of you being discovered. Go home to the girls and *when* I finish this shit I'll come back." A beat of silence passes before he finally speaks again.

"You listen and you listen well, *little brother*." Hearing those two words from his mouth has a lump forming in my throat and tears welling in my eyes. "One thing you need to learn is, Murdoch's don't leave each other behind. Murdoch's stick together till the fucking bitter end. It is our greatest strength but also our greatest weakness at the same time."

I don't know why I do it but I can't hold in this secret any longer, if I don't make it out alive I need them to know. "Rook is alive." The sharp intake of breath from the other end of the phone tells me he heard me loud and clear. "I can't explain everything right now but the Bratva have Rook. I'll get his whereabouts out of her. If shit goes south, you find Rook and save him." I decide to tell them something else I learned since I'm apparently in the mood to share secrets. "Mav hired Vin to kill Car. Tony also knew he was a rat. He brought Mav in as part of the deal with Vlad. He had to teach Mav everything but you ruined that plan when you shot him." I can hear the other three in the background shouting and promising to kill me, hurt me, help me blah blah blah. I ignore them as I wait for Bishop to speak. I know I fucked up by keeping this secret from them but I had no choice!

"Why are you telling me this now?" At the sound of Bishop's voice the other three quieten down. I know now that I'm on speakerphone, so I speak to all of them and hope like hell they will forgive me for not coming to them sooner.

"I should have told you when I first found out but I couldn't. Then when I finally saw you all at the fight I couldn't do it. I didn't want to give you false hope."

"How do you know he's alive?" Comes from Knight.

"Anya gave me a picture of him," I answer honestly.

"What did you see in the picture?" I want to lie and tell Bishop he looked well and safe but I don't.

"He was chained up, blood and dirt covering him, he... he looked terrified, Bish." Chaos erupts from their side, I can hear things being smashed and shouts ensue.

"Give me that!" Is all I hear before King is barking down the phone. "Fuck the Bratva, fuck that bitch, your one job is to find the whereabouts of our brother. I don't give a fuck about anything else. You find Rook, Gage, and don't fucking ever hide shit like this again!" he roars down the line before he ends the call.

"Fuck!" I mutter beneath my breath before scrubbing a hand down my face. I knew they were going to be pissed but I didn't expect them to be this mad. The fact Bishop didn't rebuke King tells me that he agrees. He wants our brother home safe more than he wants to end the Bratva.

But what if I can do both?

Laying here next to Anya with my arms wrapped around her, a deep ache begins to form in my chest. I lied not only to my brothers but to her as well. The first night she came to me and gave me the picture of Rook wasn't the first time I've seen her. I watched her come and go from the club for weeks. She always came in with a vibrant determined look in her eyes, when she left she always looked defeated and beaten down. A few times I spotted bruises on her arms, legs and face. Now though, I can feel it in the pit of my gut that those bruises weren't always from her fighting in the cage.

My hold on her tightens. I pull her in closer and love feeling her naked body pressed against my own. When I finally made it into the room with our dinner, we ate in silence then she lead to me to the shower where she stripped us both, then gave me the best fucking blow job of my life. Of course, I had to return the favor numerous times and make sure she was sated and knew that her pleasure belonged to me. I told her that until I leave Russia, my cock would be the only one, she would be coming on, but the truth is, each time I bury myself in her heat, the need I feel for her grows rather than lessens. When the time comes, will I be able to let her go?

I startle slightly when she speaks, I thought she was asleep. "Tomorrow, you need to act like nothing has happened between us. The Crows don't view me as a person, they see me as Vlad's heir and assume I want what he does. You cannot show them that you care for me, Gage, they need to think you hate me."

"I don't give a fuck what people think, killer." She rolls over in my hold and cups my cheek with her tiny hand, her eyes are filled with anguish.

"I'm getting that but this isn't about you. If anyone

knows I mean something to you they will use me to get to you." Not wanting to acknowledge the knot that is forming in my chest from her words, I decide to change the subject all together.

"Why have you not spoken to Koby?"

"Why do you care?" she counters with a slight bite to her tone.

"Because she is... well I guess her, Ally and Kiara are like best friends–no, they're more like sisters to me. Her not hearing from you really fucked her up. She thought you had died." She takes a shuddering breath and closes her eyes as if she's in pain.

"Someone did die, but it wasn't me," she whispers, agony is clear in her tone. I tighten my hold on her and place a tender kiss to her forehead, somehow this conversation has transported us from just fucking to–more than fucking?

"What is that supposed to mean?" I ask.

"I don't regret for a second helping Dimitri and Katarina–sorry, Koby escape Russia. I just wish saving one friend didn't cost me another but I wasn't that fortunate." I can see the pain etched on her beautiful face and I want to wipe that look off her and never see it again. "My cousin, Dante, he is... was Alek's younger brother, was murdered by my father. Vlad blamed him for his wife being able to flee and because I wouldn't give up her location, he made Dante pay the price for my sins." The pieces all come together for me now.

"You didn't call because you knew he would be watching you and waiting for you to contact her so he could hunt her down?" She burrows her face against my chest and nods. Fuck, this girl has been through as much shit as my family and yet she somehow is able to still see the good in the world. I make a promise to myself right here, when I leave Russia, I'm not leaving her behind.

"Losing Dante changed me but what Vlad did next destroyed me," she mumbles against my chest.

"What did he do?" I growl out, knowing full well that whatever she says is going to fucking sting like a bitch.

"After they fled, he beat me unconscious which wasn't something new." My hold on her tightens to the point I know it will bruise but can't find it within myself to care right now. "I woke up in a clinic, I was so confused about how I had gotten there. When a nurse finally came in I begged her to tell me what happened, her and two other nurses ignored me until Ivan finally came in later that after-noon. I'll never forget the happy look on his face or the smile he wore when he told me that Vlad had ordered a hysterectomy be performed, so that I would never be able to give his future enemy he would marry me off to an heir." I'm so shocked that I open and close my mouth several times wanting to say something but not knowing what the right thing is to say. *I'm sorry* doesn't seem like it would be wise to say. "My own father, my own fucking blood took away any chance I would ever have at becoming a mother. Earlier, you said you wanted kids and I shut down because I will never be able to have that luxury in the future. I will die never knowing what it's like to create a life and nurture it inside me until it's time for it to come into this fucking shitty world."

I feel her tears against my chest and it fucking destroys me to hear her story and know that I won't be able to fix this for her. Nothing anyone would do can change the outcome of this situation. Vladimir robbed his own fucking daughter of the chance to become a mother and experience what it might be like to carry a life inside her.

"Your father is a cunt, what he did to you is... I don't even have words. I swear to you, Anya, I will not leave Russia until your father is dead. I know that will never atone for what he has taken from you but I hope that maybe, just maybe his death will start the process of you being able to heal." I have no fucking idea where the hell that came from but judging from the way she relaxes fully into me, it was the right thing to say. She pulls back and stares up at me with a timid watery smile.

"For someone who doesn't want to care or shouldn't care, you sure seem like you do." I scoff.

"I never said I didn't care, I just said I shouldn't. Somehow you seem to have given me a reason to *want* to care and that is something I haven't done in a really long fucking time."

"When this is all over, I wish... I wish that you would stay and give me a chance to really know you." Instead of fucking her all night like I had to planned to, we find ourselves talking and sharing memories and stories from our past. It feels so weird to share stories of how I grew up and not be judged but I guess it's the same for her. Both of us haven't had an easy life, but because of that, we both know that we will never settle for less than what we know we deserve.

Chapter Twenty

Anya

I've been a nervous wreck since we dropped Vor and Gage off at some run-down dive bar where they will meet with someone who will take Gage to the Crows' hideout. Worrying about someone other than myself is new to me and I don't know if I like it. I have only ever been concerned for three people in my life: one of them is dead and the other two are on the run from my father. Gage Matthews has managed to weasel his way inside me and as much as I want to say I hate it—I don't. Last night was the first time in my twenty-one years of life where I felt free to speak freely and just be me. Last night Gage didn't just listen, he *heard* everything I said to the point he would cut in and refer back to something I said earlier, that is something so new to me.

Krill pulls up out front of the club. It makes me sick to

see the line of people that span down the street trying to get in. They have no idea what goes on at the back of this club. Some of the girls in this line have no fucking clue that they won't be leaving here tonight if they catch the attention of one of the captains or worse, my father and uncle's attention. Krill parks the car next to the curb, everyone is staring hoping to catch a glimpse of who is inside. Krill opens my door, not bothering to offer me a hand. He knows the rules, he cannot show me any type of kindness as per Vlad's orders. I hold my head high and ignore everyone as I walk toward the entrance with Krill right behind me. Ishta opens the red rope with a curt nod of his head letting me through. We pass the first door only to be stopped by Koba. I grit my teeth when the piece of shit runs his hands all over my body, searching me for weapons.

"Ona chistaya," (*she's clean*) he calls to the new guard behind him I don't recognize. He opens the door and immediately the bass from the music booms. The stench of sweat and body odor permeates my nasal passages and I quickly breath through my mouth as we move forward. Koba darts his arm out stopping us. Krill steps forward pushing me behind him. He may not be able to show me kindness but his job is to make sure I am not harmed–it's comical really. If Vlad wants to beat me Krill is made to stand back and watch. "Boss khochet yeye videt." (*The boss wants to see her*)

Krill doesn't respond, just turns and motions for me to lead the way to my father's office. I keep my face blank and head high as I make my way through the packed club. People move out of the way as if they can sense the danger that clings to me. It's almost like they have a sixth sense that if they get too close, the stench of death that clings to me will rub off on them. Nerves thrum through me the closer I get to the back of the bar where the door that will lead me to my father's office waits. The guard sees me approaching and swipes his key card, pushing it open. I don't stop, just continue through the dimly lit hall past all of the fucking red doors. I hate the color red. I hate this place. I hate everything it fucking stands for and what happens behind these fucking doors. I turn left and keep walking with poise knowing they are watching me on the cameras that litter this place. They want to see me squirm and I refuse to give them the satisfaction.

I stop in front of his office door, it's red like the others but not the same shade. His door seems darker, more foreboding then the others, almost like a shadow has been cast over it. I know I should knock but what's the point when he has summoned me. He knows I'm here so I throw caution to the wind and open the door. I take one step inside and pause, six guns trained on me. I don't cower, I look to each of the six captains and wait for them to either grow the balls and pull that fucking trigger or lower their guns. Vlad sits behind his desk with a gleeful smile on his face, the thought of watching me bleed out always brings a smile to his weathered, evil old face.

"Uberi ikh, ona ne ugroza." (*Put them away, she is no threat*) The sound of Ivan's voice draws my attention to the back of the room, where he sits in a wingback chair in front of the fire with a glass of vodka in his hand. His eyes bore into me, and I fight the shiver of unease that crawls through me. He sits there like he is a king in an expensive Armani suit, salt and pepper colored hair slicked back against his head, his green eyes burning with bloodlust. Ivan has a scar that runs from the edge of his jaw all the way to his ear. He got that scar from Dante and Alek's mother. Needless to say, no one ever heard from my aunt after that day.

"Ostav' nas!" (*Leave us!*) Vlad barks. Slowly the captains lower their guns, nod to Vlad and exit the room. Not before shoulder checking me on their way past. I grit my teeth and bare their resentment knowing they hate me because regardless of how Vlad views me, they know I will always rank higher because of who I am to Vlad. Once the room is clear, I step forward but halt at Vlad's next words that send a pit of dread pooling inside me. "Get out, Krill." I keep my face blank of emotion and pray to god Vlad can't see the fear that I am feeling in my eyes.

"Da, Pakhan," Krill mutters before I hear the door close behind him. The room is bathed in tension-filled silence. I don't take my eyes off my father even when I hear Ivan stand and move toward us. Vlad and I have the same shaped face, the same cupid's bow and even the same nose, but what I don't have is his dark death-filled brown eyes. I have my mother's eyes and he hates it. Vlad's hair is starting to gray on the sides and it drives him mad knowing that even he, the great Pakhan, can't stop his own aging. I fight the gasp that wants to break free when I feel Ivan at my back. He leans down and runs his nose along the column of my exposed neck and inhales.

"You smell so fucking sweet." He smacks his lips together to drive his point home. Having dealt with his sexual innuendos for years, I know it's better to just stand here and take it. I almost whimper when he reaches around and cups my tit, squeezing it to the point of pain. I hold my father's gaze hoping that he will stop this, I fucking hate myself for thinking he would ever come to my aide. "Hmmmm, God, I bet your pussy is so fucking tight." I can't fight the shiver of disgust that rolls through, that one mistake is going to cost me. I can see it in Vlad's eyes when he stands from his chair, he looks over my shoulder to speak directly to my uncle.

"Take my daughter to your playroom, you have an hour to do... whatever you like before I come for answers." Everything inside me stills, I swear even my heart stops. Ivan's dark chuckle can barely be heard over the blood roaring in my ears. Vlad has punished me in the past for fucking up, but he has never allowed to Ivan harm me. Sure he knows that his brother is a sick fuck and wants in my pants but he has never let him off his leash. The hatred that shines in my father's eyes as he looks at me tells me he knows—he knows I have betrayed him and will use me to get the answers he needs in order to take down the Murdoch family. "You disgust me, Anya. You spread you fucking legs like a whore. You're exactly like your mother. You are worthless, the only thing you had going for you was your untouched cunt and even that is ruined now." I open my mouth to rebuke his claim but he pushes on. "You really think I didn't have my whole house under surveillance? I saw you with that American bastard. You spread your legs so fucking easily like a good whore, now you will do the same for my brother."

"Papa, please–" I don't even get to finish begging before something smacks me over the back of the head and everything goes dark as I fall to the ground hoping that I won't wake up. That would be the better outcome than what Ivan will do to me.

Chapter Twenty-One

Gage

Vor and I stand beside each other in an old gym, the bleachers are broken and the basketball hoops are missing from the boards. Graffiti decorates every wall, the stench of piss is strong and has me wanting to gag so I breathe through my mouth. After Krill and Anya dropped us off, we were transported here by two guys that are in the Crows. I don't trust any of these fuckers, which is why I have a bug from Vin in my pocket and managed to get one on Anya without her knowing. At least this way if shit goes south, my brother's and Vin will be able to find us and hear everything that is said. Anya may think she can handle herself but Vlad is a wildcard. I wouldn't put it past him to use his own daughter to get what he wants.

"You're doing the right thing." I turn to Vor and quirk a

brow in question. I don't trust this fucker. "You wouldn't be able to go against Vlad on your own–"

"We have back up, we don't need you," I sneer. He shrugs his shoulders and wiggles his brows at me which just serves to piss me off.

"How would they get in since Vlad has the whole country on lock down? All the borders are closed, airports are monitored around the clock so anyone that was coming to aide you would never make it in."

I smirk. "You've never met Tony Bennett, believe me, when Bishop calls, Tony will find a way in and help his future son-in-law end this fucking pathetic war."

"I know of Tony Bennett. I also know about your family and what you and your brothers have achieved in your country. But you are a fool to doubt Vlad's reach. He owns Russia, Gage. The schools, hospitals, clubs, airports, police, army... I could go on and on but you wouldn't grasp the severity of this situation. We know Russia and we know how the Bratva operates. Allow us to help you end this and I swear to you that you will have an ally in the Crows."

"Yeah?" He nods like a fucking idiot. "Who gave you the permission to offer that deal because we both know you don't rank high enough to offer me shit!"

"I gave him the permission." Both Vor and I turn toward the doors in the back and my fucking jaw unhinges at the sight of the man. He's flanked by two guys I haven't seen before and walks toward us with a swagger only a dead man could pull off. He stops a foot away from me, we size each other up but my mind is still reeling at the fact he is *alive!*

"You're supposed to be dead!" I deadpan. He just smiles and nods to Vor and the others, the three of them exit the gym leaving the two of us alone.

"I should have been. Anya Volkov is stronger than she

looks. That girl can pack a fucking punch." That brings a proud smile to my face, my girl knows how to handle herself. "She gave me a choice."

"And what choice was that, *Andreas*?" He doesn't look pissed at the way I spat his name, he just seems... at ease?

"Allow her to shove a pill in my mouth that would slow my pulse and heart rate making everyone think I was dead, or she would actually kill me." I can't keep the surprised look off my face. "Oh, she didn't tell you?" It pisses me off to admit that she didn't but I understand why she kept this to herself.

"That's why Vor and Krill offered to help her, isn't it?" I ask.

"Yes. She proved she wasn't like her father when she let the leader of her enemy live. Anya will be spared in this war but her kin will not. Ivan, Alek and Vlad will all pay with their lives." The conviction in his tone has me believing him.

"Why are you doing this? I get you hate the Bratva but you had a chance to disappear and leave Russia. Why stay?" His eyes take on a faraway look and I can tell he is reliving a memory.

"The story I tell everyone is that the Bratva turned my girlfriend into an addict and put her on the block." I screw my face up in disgust. "The real reason I started the Crows and the reason why I want them all dead is because Dante Volkov was my best friend and..." He trails off allowing me to put the pieces together.

"Holy fuck, you were in love with Anya's cousin?" He doesn't cringe or deny my claim.

"Dante wasn't like his father or brother... He was good and kind. He wasn't made for this life and he paid the fucking price for being born into this fucking life. I vowed to get revenge for him years ago and I am a man of my word. You're here, Gage, because we could use the help of your family and the connections they have to overthrow the Bratva."

"What exactly are you asking of me?" I eye him warily waiting for him to reveal his true motives.

"I'm offering your family a safe harbor here with the Crows until we take down Vladimir. Help me and I swear to you there will never be a skin trade in Russia again. On my honor, you have my word no Crow will harm Anya Volkov or ever come after her for the crimes of her father and uncle." I clench my hands into fists at my sides and grit my teeth in anger.

"You so much as *think* of touching her and I'll kill you with the fucking pen in my pocket." He throws his head back and laughs, then claps me on the shoulder and motions for me to follow him. This guy is fucking nuts!

<hr>

I'm fucking wrecked and dead on my feet, I have learned so much about the Crows and how they operate. I thought they were just some punk street gang trying to play with the big boys but I was so fucking wrong. The Crows have men on the inside of the Bratva, politician's here and throughout the world. They own shares in banks, hotels, pharmacies, schools, you name it they probably own half of it. They run under a shell cooperation that leads back to offshore companies that can't be traced back to them. Andreas might be right, they might just be as good as the Bratva, if not better.

"So, you see now why we can overthrow them? They may have the cops and the army but they don't own them all." Andreas and his men haven't been buying people like

Vlad, they have been tracking down family members that have been trafficked and returning them. They don't need to buy people when they earn their loyalty. "We will help you if you help us." I take a sip of the scotch Andreas poured me earlier and stare at him in a new light. He is young but somehow looks way older and younger at the same time.

"You want to do a hostile takeover to push him out of government, but how? You can't impeach him, can you?" He reclines back in the suede couch and rests his arm over the back. He seems so at ease. We're sitting in his office that looks nothing like the gym I was in earlier. They decided to leave the outside of the building and all the main rooms run down and destroyed while they remodeled the basement and set it up as their headquarters. I must say, when we came down here, I didn't expect it to look so... nice. Andreas shoots me a dark smirk, the cunning glint in his eyes sets me on edge.

"The takeover is already in motion. The general whose daughters we saved is already preparing to take over leadership of the Russian army. The officers we have on our side are already making moves to clear out Vlad's guys. The hotels, clubs and all his other dealings are being dealt with as we speak." This news shocks me. While we have been playing catch up for weeks these guys are already way in front of us.

"What about the ports?" I ask. A dark look takes over his face and his lip thin into a hard line.

"The containers are being shipped, but not to America. They are being moved to Dubai where the girls will remain until this situation is resolved, then they will return. The Crows aren't just based in Russia, we are everywhere, Gage, and all we want is to end the tyranny people like Vladimir impose on us." Before I can respond a knock sounds at the door. Andreas calls out to come in. Vor walks in which doesn't surprise me but when I see who follows after him, I'm on my feet in a split second.

"What are you doing here?" I rush to say as my brothers and Vince fill the room. Bishop comes to me and claps me on the shoulder, his guarded look has dread pooling inside me, something happened.

"That was a clever move bugging Anya and yourself." Pride swells inside me, I look to the others and frown when King and Knight both refuse to meet my gaze. I look to Vin next and my stomach cramps with unease, guilt shines in his eyes and it throws me. I turn back to Bishop and flinch when he rests a hand on my shoulder.

"What the hell is going on, Bish?" I ask hesitantly. Bishop flicks his gaze to Andreas for a beat before focusing back on me.

"I'm only saying this in front of him because we heard enough today to bury him if he betrays us." I shoot Andreas a look but he doesn't seem surprised that I've been recording us this whole time and my brothers have heard everything. He just shrugs and motions with his hand for Bishop to continue saying whatever it is he was going to.

"Your girl walked right into a trap. Vlad knows she was playing him and he gave her to her uncle to... I'm sure you can piece that together for yourself." Bishop's words play over and over in my mind. I thought I would rage and break shit but instead all I feel is deep-seated worry and self-loathing. I knew I shouldn't have let her go back. I fucking knew it was too easy to get inside the boss's house and bug his office but allowed myself to think I was... better than him.

"I have to get her back. I won't let that fucker touch her, Bishop," I growl out.

"I know." His gaze implores me to listen before I shut down and go after her. "He is waiting for you to go after her. I need you to trust me–"

"Fuck you. If that was Kiara you would already be there," I snap, he doesn't get angry at me, just nods.

"I didn't realize she meant that much to you. If you're comparing her to Kiara, she must be more than a bed warmer?"

Is she?

I ponder it for a second and realize without even trying, Anya Volkov has left a mark on me. She has managed to make me feel more alive than I have felt in years. I wouldn't go as far as to say I love her... wait, do I? Fucked if I know but what I do know is I need to get her back and find out if what this *thing* is between us is the real deal.

"She's my girl and I want her back," I say leaving no room for argument.

Chapter Twenty-Two

I gasp awake when a bucket of water is thrown on me. I try to move back but flinch in pain. My hands are handcuffed above my head and my feet are shackled to the floor. Fear uncurls inside me. I dart my gaze around the room and freeze at the sight of a pale Alek sitting in a seat in the corner, looking at me with nothing but hatred, but I find comfort in seeing him arm in a sling from being shot. The sound of a bucket hitting the concrete floor on my other side draws my attention. Ivan stands there with a bright smile on his face. He has a rubber apron on and bright blue rubber gloves. My fear turns to panic when Ivan's gaze runs down my body. I follow his movement and fight back a whimper when I see I'm in my red lace bra and matching thong. I bite down on the inside of my cheek to keep my tears at bay. He stripped me and that can only mean one thing.

"I hope you don't mind, darling, but I thought my son might like to watch." It's posed as a question but I know Ivan, he never asks for permission *or* forgiveness, he does as he likes, consequences be damned. "Now, we can do this the hard way or the harder way, you choose?" I close my eyes and take a deep breath trying to calm myself, when I open my eyes again Ivan has moved closer and only a foot separates us.

"What is it you want to know, uncle?" A dark glimmer enters his eyes and I know with every fiber of my being I am not getting out of this fucking room–wherever *this* room may be–unscathed. He reaches out and runs a glove covered finger down the gap between my breasts. It takes everything inside me not to jerk away from his touch when he boldly cups my left tit in his hand.

"I want to know everything," he whispers the words like a lover would. "I want to know what you know about the Americans and where they are. Then you are going to tell me who shot my son." His grip on my breast becomes painful as he squeezes it hard, this time I can't fight the flinch. "After that, I'm going to destroy you in the best way possible." He leans toward me, I jerk back against my restraints to keep our distance but he uses his other hand to grip my hair and yank my head back, drawing a sharp cry from me. He darts his tongue out and licks a path from the base of my neck to the shell of my ear. I shudder in disgust. He clamps his teeth down on my lobe causing me to scream out in pain, I fear he may bite it off until he draws back at the last minute. I see blood on his bottom lip, my blood. The sick fuck darts his tongue out to lick the blood from his lip and moans.

"Can you save that shit for after I'm gone?" Alek says, sounding bored. I look at him and feel nothing but contempt. I wish it was him that died and not Dante. Alek is a carbon copy of his father and mine. Vlad has always wished that Alek was his son because of how cruel he is. Alek didn't need to be trained or taught how to be a tyrant, he was born like that. Ivan rolls his eyes dramatically, almost like he finds humor in this whole situation.

"Fine, let's get to it." He takes a step back and smiles so bright, which has me fearing for my life worse than I was before. "Bring it in!" he calls out. At the sound of a door opening I turn and peer over my shoulder and watch the heavy metal door push open. I watch a skinny bronzed skin man who keeps his head down push in a cart with a white sheet covering its contents. He pushes the cart near the wall, then steps back against the wall keeping his head down. Something about the man seems so familiar but I can't pinpoint where I would know him from. His body is littered with bruises and cuts, he is filthy and in serious need of a haircut. When Vlad moves toward the cart the man begins to tremble in fear which causes Vlad to laugh.

Vlad pulls the white sheet off the cart and holds it out to the man to grab, when he does he lifts his head for the first time and I gasp drawing his gaze to mine. My eyes are wide with surprise and dread. I thought he was dead! Vlad had told me they killed him when the Murdoch's took out the last two remaining families!

"Rook..." I breathe. His eyes widen a fraction before he drops his chin to his chest and steps back against the wall. Ivan looks from Rook to me with a cruel glint in his eyes. He reaches out and claps Rook on the shoulder causing him to flinch in both fear and pain. The photo I gave Gage was one taken a couple weeks after Rook arrived. I found it in Vlad's office and knew that picture would come in handy one day. And it did. Guilt has been eating at me daily because I thought he was dead and knowing the only reason Gage was helping me was because he thought I had his brother. From the look of the youngest Murdoch, death would have been better than whatever he has suffered through.

"He doesn't go by that name anymore, he goes by *Dvornyaga (mutt)*" My chest constricts when Rook lifts his head to look at Ivan, this poor boy has been beaten into submission so much so that at the mention of his *name,* he is standing at attention. His handsome face is caked with filth and covered by a beard. He looks like he was a muscular guy at one time and now he is nothing but skin and bone. I can see the guy's fucking ribcage! "Kneel!" Ivan commands. Rook drops to the concrete floor in front of his master and waits like a fucking dog. Ivan looks at me and wiggles his brows.

"What the hell have you done to him?" I shout, I'm too focused on Ivan to notice that Alek has moved until my head jerks back from the force of his hit. I cry out when he lands another blow to my stomach. I gag and slump in my chains as I gasp for air. Alek doesn't care, he yanks on my hair pulling my head back only to back hand me. Tears threaten to spill but I manage to keep them at bay. I lose the fight when he reels his arm back and punches me right in the nose, breaking it. I scream out as blood begins to rush down my chin. My head is yanked back again, this time he doesn't hit me, just spits right in my face.

"Ty sdokhnesh', gryaznaya shlyukha, ty trakhnul nashu sem'yu v posledniy raz, suka!" (*You're going to die you filthy whore, you fucked our family over for the last time you bitch!*) Alek sneers. He's so close, I can feel his breath fanning across my face so I do the only thing I can, I rear my head back and headbutt him right in the fucking nose, returning the favor of breaking his nose. He stumbles back and cups his nose with his hand. I relish in his agony. "You fucking bitch!" he roars in anger then tears his sling off. I brace myself for what is about to happen. No matter how prepared you are, you can never fully prepare yourself to block out the pain. Alek lands blow after blow to my face, ribs, stomach. I can feel the cuffs cutting into my wrists from being jerked in every direction from the hits. My throat is hoarse from screaming out in pain. When black spots begin to dance in my vision, I welcome the blackness with open arms.

The feeling of rocking rouses me, immediately I wish I was still unconscious because the pain is excruciating. I feel myself being jostled and will my eyes to open but they refuse. I flinch in pain when I feel tears begin to leak from my eyes before I open them. My ears register the sounds of grunts coming from above me. I blink my eyes open and whimper. I turn away from Ivan and see my arms are anchored either side of me by leather cuffs to a wooden table. I flinch again when he slams his cock inside me. Tears flow freely down my cheeks. He reaches down and yanks the cups of my bra down drawing another whimper from me, then squeezes my nipples so hard I cry out.

"That's it, scream for me like the fucking whore you are!" The breathy tone of his voice has bile rushing up my throat. I turn away from the wall and chuck up the breakfast I ate. The table is too wide so my vomit sits there, right next to my face as if mocking me. Movement catches my eye and I see Rook kneeling in the corner, his gaze fixated on mine. I try to detach myself from what is happening to my body and focus on Rook and the anguish in his gaze, but the moment Ivan pulls out of me, I'm brought back to the present. Ivan moves toward the cart Rook brought in earlier with his hard cock swinging. I fight to not spew again at the sight of his skinny pathetic cock. I fight against my restraints but it's useless. Ivan grabs a wrench and spins back to face me.

I stare at him in horror, he stands there completely naked and unashamed that Rook is eye level with his cock. He must see something in my eyes because he smiles as he reaches down and pats Rook's head. He flinches from Ivan's touch but doesn't pull away. Ivan keeps his gaze on me the whole time, a sick feeling churns inside me as his smile grows.

"Suck." He says that one word and Rook tenses but swivels around so he is kneeling with his back to me. I watch Rook's head bob up and down on Ivan's cock. Bile rises again but this time I fight it back. Anger, disgust and hatred like I have never felt before comes to life inside me. I can't stand to watch Gage's brother be humiliated and used like this by my own kin, so I do something I never thought I ever would.

"How pathetic." The smile on Ivan's face vanishes. He grips Rook's hair and yanks him back causing him to fall backward. "You use that fucking mafia piece of shit to get you off." I scoff in an effort to drive my point home. Ivan's grip on the wrench tightens to the point his knuckles turn white. "I always knew you couldn't get off on Russian pussy, I just had no idea it took a half-beaten *cock* to get you hard."

Chapter Twenty-Three

Anya

I'm still writhing in pain from Ivan fucking me with the wrench, my pussy is burning and fucking sore but that hasn't stopped him from shoving his cock inside it or in my mouth. The worst was when he ordered Rook to come help him flip me over and hold my ass cheeks open while he fucked it. I screamed so loud and long that I passed out from either the pain or lack of oxygen. I can't stop shaking, pain is radiating throughout my body. I've cried so much that now I have no tears left. Rook hasn't been able to look at me since he helped Ivan. Truth is, I don't blame Rook for any of this.

"Here it is." The gleeful sound of Ivan's voice has me tensing. He spins away from the cart and waves a thin strip of bamboo and a hammer. I try to keep the confusion from my face, I don't want to give him the satisfaction. I know I have been with him longer than an hour but I haven't had the nerve to ask where my father is or where Alek went. No amount of training or fighting in the cage could have prepared me for this. Ivan stalks toward me, still naked and fucking hard! The sick cunt downed some Viagra to keep him *ready for me,* he said.

Ivan whistled as he made his way over to me, he gripped my hand and held it flat, I tried to yank it free but couldn't thanks to his hold and the restraints. He called out to Rook, who ambled over slowly with a look of shame and guilt shinning in his dark eyes. I plead with my eyes hoping that he will help me—help us both by using some of those tools on the cart to take Ivan out. Rook takes Ivan's place and holds my hand flat. Ivan places the thin piece of Bamboo beneath my fingernail, my eyes widen in horror when he uses the hammer to smash the bamboo forward. I scream out so loud the sound rings in my own ears, and tears I thought I no longer could cry fall from my eyes. Agony. That is the only word to describe the feeling of having something smashed under your nail, I can feel the bamboo right up to my cuticle.

"Now, answer my question and I won't do that to your other fingers." I grit my teeth and breathe through my nose trying to control my urge to lash out and call him every name under the sun. "Where is your boyfriend and his brother's?" I give him the answer Gage and I had discussed.

"He's with the Crows, he's a mole for them." I gasp out trying not to focus on the pain, pretty hard when my whole fucking body is in pain. Ivan clicks his tongue and shakes his head as he yanks the bamboo out from under my nail. I cry out. He lines it up with my next finger and I begin to thrash against my restraints. "I told you what you wanted to know!" I scream out, and he grips my chin in a bruising grip.

"You're a fucking liar." His eyes burn with a look so dark I can't think of a word to describe it. "You gave him up too easy and after watching the videos from your father's house..." He tsks before continuing, "You wouldn't give him up that easy. I saw the way you looked at him, darling, you love him." My eyes widen and I try to shake my head to deny his claim but he just tightens his grip causing me to wince. "I saw the look in your eyes, Anya, your mind may not know it but your heart does. You fell in love with our enemy but not to worry because he feels the same and he will come for you."

The only sounds, for the next hour or however long it is, that can be heard is my screams. I even resorted to begging. He has nailed a piece of bamboo under each of my fingers and toes, I would take getting beaten over and over again rather than have him do that again. I can't even twitch my fingers or toes without searing pain erupting everywhere. I sniffle and close my eyes not wanting to see what he does next. No matter the answer I gave to his questions, he didn't believe me. I even told the truth by the end. I knew then, it didn't matter what answer I gave, Ivan wouldn't believe me. He just wanted to believe I was lying so he could continue to hurt me for his own sick pleasure. My body is spent and my mind is exhausted. I wish I could black out from the pain again just to rest for a while.

"The sight of you bloody, bruised and broken has my cock gleaming with pre-cum." I close my eyes and ignore him, what's the point in fighting when he is going to rape me again and there's nothing I do can stop him. I hoped Rook would man up and help me. Fuck, Ivan was the one who shot him so I thought he may at least want some type of revenge, but no, he's been beaten into the perfect little pet. I feel Ivan step between my shackled legs, I tense instinctively and regret it when pain reverberates throughout my body. "Hmm, your pussy is beautiful covered in blood. Mind if I have a taste?" I shudder at the thought but remain silent. He grips the insides of my thighs in a punishing grip that I know will leave bruises. When I feel the first swipe of his tongue a soft cry tumbles from my lips.

I've been beaten and thrown into fights I had no business fighting in when I've pissed Vlad off, or just because he wanted to see me beaten and hurt—but never has he ever allowed something like this to happen. At the sound of the metal door opening, a small whimper escapes me. Ivan jumps to his feet and turns slightly pale. I tilt my head back to see who is able to inspire such a look like that on my uncle. Confusion wars inside me when I see Krill and Vlad standing in the doorway. Vlad looks furious, Krill tries to mask his anger but fails when his gaze connects with mine.

"Kakogo khrena ty delayesh'?" (*What the fuck are you doing?*) Vlad demands. Ivan huffs in annoyance but doesn't move from between my legs.

"Getting answers," Ivan says it like this is something natural and acceptable.

"Why the fuck is she strapped to a table and naked? And why the fuck is your cock out?" Vlad yells. Vlad never loses his cool like this. I'm so fucking confused, he told Ivan he had an hour with me and I know for a fucking fact it has been at least a day or more since I've been with him. The bastard has been snorting coke so he can stay up and *enjoy* his time as he put it.

"Beating her wasn't working. She begged me to fuck her so I couldn't say no. Fuck her pussy is so tight it strangled the fuck out of my cock." To drive his point home Ivan licks his lips and hums.

"Get the fuck out now!" Vlad shouts. Ivan shoots me a

wink then blows me a kiss as he struts from the room naked as the day he was born, without a care that anyone could see him. Vlad turns his gaze to me and for a second, one split second, I swear I see remorse in his gaze but the look is gone so fast I couldn't be sure.

"Clean her up then bring her to my office," he says to Krill before storming out of the room. As soon as Vlad is out of the room and the door shuts behind him, Krill rushes to my side. I open my mouth to thank him but he pins me with a warning look and mouths *cameras*. I clamp my mouth closed waiting for him to undo my restraints. Once I'm free, he gently grips my arm and helps me into a sitting position. I bite down that hard on my bottom lip to stop the screams from tearing free, so hard that I draw blood. He gently helps me move my legs over the edge of the table, shucks off his jacket and drapes it around my shoulders. His eyes are soft and filled with pity, but when he speaks his voice is firm and hard.

"I'll help you to your feet then you shower and be ready. Don't fuck around or keep the Pakhan waiting." My bottom lip trembles and the lump in my throat stops me from being able to speak, so I nod instead. He helps me to my feet and my legs give way. He catches me before I can fall to the ground. Pain reverberates throughout my body, black spots swarm in my vision. Before I can warn Krill that I'm going to pass out, it's too late. I become dead weight in his arms.

Chapter Twenty-Four

Gage

Three days....

I've sat by and waited for a plan to form, a plan that would get my girl back, but each time we think we have a solid one some obstacle pops up forcing us to rethink the plan and start over. Vor went back two days ago and we haven't heard a word from him or Krill. Andreas assures us that is normal but I have a sinking feeling in my gut that something fucking bad has happened. Bishop told me what they heard Vlad say to Anya, and I just know, whatever she is going through is fucking bad, worse than I could imagine, I'm sure. I look around the room, Knight and Vin sit at a desk on their computers. King is on the phone to the general that works with the Crows. Bishop and Andreas as well as half a dozen other guys stand around a table with the blue prints of Vlad's club where we know Anya is being held. Andreas has had his men scattered around the city. He has men tailing all Vlad's captains and other high ranking members.

"Dre, we have incoming," Brock, one of Andreas's computer guys, says as he nods toward the ninety-inch monitor that hangs on the wall. We all watch as Vor storms toward the gym with a bleak look on his face. I'm racing out of the room to meet him, ignoring everyone's shouts to come back. Just as I reach the door that will lead me to the flight of stairs that reach the gym, I'm tackled into the wall. I throw my hands ready to pummel the fucker but pause when I see it's Knight.

"What the fuck was that?" I shout as I shove him back a step, only for him to crowd me again.

"You can't run off half-cocked, you dick. Vor took a detour because he was followed. If you ran up there you would have given us away!"

"You fucking—wait, what?" Knight shakes his head then pins me with an annoyed look.

"When you ran out another car pulled in behind him."

"Fuck!" I snarl as I scrub a hand down my face in frustration. Knight pats me on the shoulder and his eyes soften a smidge.

"Believe it or not, we all know how you feel in a certain way. When Ally was taken, we all felt it, King more so of course, but I swear, Gage, we'll get your girl back. And then, we can finally go home and I can see my fucking girl and be there for the birth of my kids. But I need him, Gage, I can't leave here without him." Hearing him talk about Koby and their twins has guilt settling inside me.

"I won't leave Russia until we get Rook back. We'll get them both back and I swear to God you won't miss the birth of the twins. I won't let you," I say with a smile.

"Neither will I." We both turn to see Bishop and King standing in the hallway wearing looks of unease. Bish focuses his gaze on me and I stiffen. "Vor's gone. He sent a message letting us know he's being tailed and Krill is with Anya." I can tell from the way his left eye is twitching that he is holding back.

"What else?" I press. Bish takes a deep breath before continuing.

"Vor said we need to make a move within a day or Anya will die. She has been her uncle's captive for the past three days. According to Andreas, Ivan is worse than Vlad. I want that fucker's head on a pike for what he did to our brother, so we move tonight."

My emotions threaten to take hold of me as pictures of her bloodied and broken on the floor flash through my mind. I push those pictures aside and latch onto my anger. I need to keep focused until I get her in my arms, then I can lose control and tear her fucking uncle and father apart piece by fucking piece for touching what is mine. Make no fucking mistake, here and now I will admit it, Anya Volkov is mine. No one hurts what is mine and gets to live.

———

We all stand around the table with the blueprints. Andreas and at least twelve of his guys stand on the end. We have almost a dozen phones scattered around the table with other members of his crew listening in, waiting for their orders. Bishop stepped outside to call Tony, having Tony's guys here would make it three to one but there isn't enough time to fly them in. Bishop called hoping Tony would have friends here or near the borders to help us. The odds aren't good but I guess Bish had to try. Truth is, we have the element of surprise on our side and the Bratva has no idea that the Crows have infiltrated their armies and police force. With the plan we have they won't have a chance to call for backup. We'll be inside their club before they can call the troops in to help them.

"...Alek is also back with them." I tune back into the conversation at the mention of Mav, there is a special place in hell for that motherfucker! Andreas disclosed that he has three men that work for the same network as Vin and he was able to confirm that Mav was definitely the one to order the hit on my sister. If it had been anyone else that accepted the job and not Vin, Carlina would be dead.

"He's mine!" King growls. We have also learned that Mav was the one to give up Ally's location to Mikey and Donny. King has been white knuckling the edge of the table for an hour trying to tame his anger. If I was in his situation, I would be feeling the same.

"We focus on getting in first," Andreas says cutting me, Knight, King and Vin a look. "I know each of you have your reasons for wanting to kill each of them but–"

Knight cuts Andreas off. "There is no *buts*. We are the ones granting you access to the US to expand your businesses, we're also the ones gaining you a foothold in the casino chains in China, Japan, Soul and Australia. Don't think for a second because you have the manpower and we don't at this moment we are weak." My brows jump to my hairline surprised as hell to hear Knight talking business. For someone who wants nothing to do with this shit, he could have fooled me.

"I forget nothing!" Andreas sneers clearly pissed off

thanks to Knight's cock-measuring contest. "With the intel you have provided for us, we have managed to move up our timeline greatly and that was enough. Everything you just stated is an extra." Believe it or not, Andreas is actually a good guy. He doesn't keep the money he makes from all his business dealings, he actually donates most of it or invests it so he can quadruple his money to then give it to local schools. Bishop enters the room with a disgruntled look on his face, tension rolls off him in waves.

"What is it?" King asks, low enough for only us to hear when Bish reaches his side. Andreas continues speaking to his crew while we converse quietly.

"Tony has people in Mongolia and China but it will take them too long to reach us before we hit Vlad. He's sending them to us anyway, with more of his guys from Miami flying out within the hour. If shit goes south, his men will be here for backup when they arrive." That should bring us comfort but it doesn't. We don't need them to do this. All we need to do is take down Vlad, Ivan and Mav, then the rest will fall into line. "I can't pull our guys or Luka away from New York, they need to be there to keep every-thing running." We all nod our understanding. "I want Vin on the building across the street watching our backs. King stays with Knight and Gage is with me, never separate." He looks each of us in the eyes as he speaks, driving his point home. "We take these fuckers down, get our brother and Gage's girl, then we get the fuck out of this country."

"Fuck yes."

"Hell yeah, brother."

"I'm ready to get back to my girl."

"I can't wait."

The four of us say at the same time. I know being away from their better halves for months has been hard for them, but we needed to do this in order to keep them safe and get Rook back. I just hope he is still alive and Anya wasn't playing me. I don't think my brothers would survive that loss for real this time. Without a body we had a bit of hope but if we find him dead, Knight will lose control and Koby isn't here to bring him back.

Chapter Twenty-Five

Anya

I refuse to sit like my father instructed, instead I stand here in a pair of Krill's sweats that I've had to roll at the waist so they would stay up and a plain long-sleeve black top, that is miles too big for me, that he found in one of the changing rooms. Even after showering I still feel dirty, my skin feels like it's crawling with bed bugs. I couldn't stomach looking at myself for too long in the mirror. My fingers and toes are strapped thanks to Krill. The bruises and cuts that mar my body are covered thanks to the clothes I wear, but my face, no amount of makeup will ever cover that mess. Ivan and Alek stand behind Vlad. I refuse to even spare them a glance, I hope they rot in hell for what they did to me!

Vlad steeples his fingers together and rests his chin atop of them. "You could have avoided all of that if you had just did as you were told." I fight the urge to roll my eyes, nothing I ever did for him managed to get me a free pass. "I want the notes and a full break down on the operation you run then... you're free to go."

"Y-you." I stop and clear my throat, cringing. It's raw and hoarse from the amount of screaming I have done. I learned from Krill that I was with Ivan for three fucking days. I managed to drink some water but still haven't eaten a single thing. I'm dizzy, tired and want nothing more than to sleep for a week. "You want me to write down how I run the drug shipments?"

Vlad's upper lip lifts in a snarl. "Yes." I nod in understanding, so this is the reason why he hasn't killed me. He needs to know how I do it before he kills me. "I want all your contact details and which flights you use." I nod, going along with this bullshit—I'm never giving him that information. "Once that is finished, I want the name of who shot your cousin, the location of your... *friend* and his family."

"Once I give you all of that, what happens to me?" I watch him carefully waiting to see the moment he lies because he will, he has lied to me every day of my life.

"You walk away and never come back."

"You'll let me go, just like that?" I push knowing full well there is no way he would ever just let me *walk away*.

"Yes," he grits out, this time I can't contain the snort that escapes me. If I'm going to die tonight, it won't be crying like a coward in the corner, it will be fighting till my last fucking breath. Vlad narrows his eyes in warning. I used to fear him, well not him directly–I feared him allowing Ivan to do what he did to me. I have nothing left to fear now. Ivan did his worst and I'm still fucking standing here.

"I always hoped and prayed that one day you would look at me like you look at Alek." Vlad grinds his teeth but I push on, I've never spoken out of turn like this before but I refuse to die never having said my piece. "Did you ever for one second in my whole life, ever care about me?" I don't give him a chance to answer. "I don't think you did, because if you had, you wouldn't have that fucking piece of shit that raped me standing beside you!" I scream. Vlad stands so fast that his chair topples over. I don't think, I just act. I turn and grab Krill's side piece from the band of his jeans, I'm too fast for him to try to stop me. I point the gun right at my father and relish in the shocked look on his face.

"Anya," Krill says my name in warning but I ignore him.

"I won't let you kill me without a fight!" I shout. I keep the three of them in my line of sight. "Any of you move and I swear on my mother's grave I will kill you where you stand."

"Your mother was a fucking whore–" A red haze overcomes me, I get tunnel vision and squeeze the trigger. The sound of the gunshot rings out in the room. Krill's Heckler and Koch side piece packs a good kick back. Vlad cries out and grips his arm that I shot. Ivan and Alek both stand there with horrified looks on their faces, neither of them can believe I just shot my father. At the sound of shouts coming from outside the room, Krill rushes to the door and flips the lock. "You fucking bitch, you shot me!"

I glare at the bastard that gave me life. "Say another bad word about my mother, I dare you!" My voice is even and I'm so fucking proud of myself when my tone doesn't waiver. I don't know what the hell has come over me. Never in my life would I ever have the balls to speak to my father this way or ever dream about holding him at gunpoint, but I guess we all have our limits and I've reached mine.

"Put the gun down." I dart my gaze to Alek, he looked so in control when I last saw him, albeit a little crazed since he was beating the shit out of me. Now, he looks spooked. "You know you won't make it out of this room alive."

"And who is going to stop me?" I spot Ivan moving his hand around his back and quickly point the gun at him, the pounding on the door doesn't deter me. "Reach for that gun and I'll put a fucking bullet in your head before you can blink." His upper lip twitches but he doesn't argue, he drops his arms back to his sides. Vlad drops back into his chair still holding the side of his arm. He's a fucking hypochondriac, it was only a flesh wound, he'll live.

"You have a choice. Put the gun down and I'll make sure you die swiftly." He doesn't bother to elaborate on another option, we all know what that option would be. I would be given to Ivan. The pounding and shouts from the other side of the door grow more frantic, I didn't really think this through.

"You have to make a call, they will break this door down, even if it is reinforced." Vlad's office has bullet proof walls and door, it will take them a while to break the door down which means I need to decide what the fuck I am going to do. "You and I both know that you don't have the *yatza's* (*balls*) to pull that trigger."

"You have no fucking idea what I am capable of, *father*," I spit the word at him like it's acid. I decide to lay all my cards on the table for the first time ever, I have never told a single soul about what I have been doing. Now is the perfect time to let them all in on my little secret.

"You think you have what it takes to be me?" I smirk at my father, for a split second his mask of indifference falters.

"Don't you know you should never doubt a woman with nothing to lose?" I run my gaze over the three of them, making sure they can see the hatred in my gaze and send them a dark smile. Ivan and Vlad look indifferent but Alek, he can see from the look in my eyes that I am about to shatter their world, he looks pale. "I don't need to be you. I'm already better than you were and greater than you ever will be. Your captains put on a good show when I first got here, but did you ever ask yourself why none of them were able to find me while I was holed up in a cabin fucking Gage Matthews brains out?" Vlad's eyes widen, Ivan the sick fuck smiles wide and it disgusts me to see pride in his eyes. Alek shakes his head trying to deny what I am saying but he can't.

"My men are fucking loyal to me!" Vlad roars.

"Oh, papa, your men *were* loyal to you. Their allegiance changed the moment you started trafficking members of their families and dragging their sisters, wives, daughters and mothers into your red rooms of fucking pain and raping them!" I'm screaming now but I don't give a fuck. I'm well past caring because I am going to kill the three of them before I walk out of this fucking room. I am the only person who can get close enough to do it. "All I had to do was whisper a few things in their ears and they promised to back me when the time came for me to dethrone to Pakhan." Vlad's eyes are wide with panic. "I may lose all the holdings you have in the businesses and political backing but I don't need it, *I* have the Bratva." I didn't have enough time or pull to get to any of the political leaders but I can worry about that later, same with the businesses. We'll take a huge loss but we can rebuild in time.

I'm too focused on watching my father's reaction to my declaration that I don't see Alek pull his gun. It's like everything happens in slow motion. I turn to him and pull the trigger the same time he does, my scream rents the air before I drop to the ground like a sack of shit.

Chapter Twenty-Six

Gage

So many different emotions course through me as we near the club—adrenalin, rage, dread, but worst of all, *hope.*

Hope she is okay.

Hope she is alive.

Hope she wasn't harmed.

Hope is the worst fucking emotion you could ever feel. Hope gets people killed. It's the one emotion that can make you do the stupidest thing and get yourself killed. I may not have realized it before but right now in this moment, I know with a hundred percent certainty that I would lay down my life for Anya if it meant she got to live and be free of her father.

"ETA two minutes, strap up and be ready," Andreas calls from the front seat. Bishop, Knight and King ride in the middle row, Brock and I are in the back, while Liam drives. Vin is already set up on the roof of the building opposite the main entrance of the club. He is the best dead shot and the only one me and my brothers trust to have our backs and clear our path inside. Vin will keep it clear so we can exit in haste and get the fuck out. "The takeover is happening now, an emergency board meeting is happening as we speak. The cops and army won't come to his aide, even if we die. Vlad will be fucked and never able to recover from this."

Andreas's words should bring me gratification but they don't. All I care about right now isn't taking Vlad down, I just need to get my girl back and then I'll be able to think straight and focus. This is new for me. I've never really worried about anyone this way except for the girls, but even then, I never felt this way. I feel responsible for Anya and making sure she is safe. With the girls, I just felt a sense of... protectiveness. I feel that with Anya as well but it's worse. I double check my guns and make sure that I have the four grenades strapped to the front of my bullet proof vest. We each have tactical helmets on to protect us from head shots —the Crows offered for us to use their Kevlar suits and guns, but we declined. We may be helping each other but that didn't mean we trusted them to not give us faulty guns, you can never trust someone who wants the same thing you do. Make no mistake, whether Andreas admits it or not, he wants to lead the Bratva and Bishop won't let that happen. He can't risk him turning out like Vlad.

When we round the corner to where the club is, everyone shifts forward in their seats. Liam slams on the breaks causing us all to jerk. We all amble out of the vehicle sluggishly, we were supposed to jump out of the car and run into the club guns blazing but instead we stand here at the curb staring. Crowds of people run from the building, some men that are with Bratva come out with bullet wounds, the smell of smoke draws my attention to the back of the club. Billows of smoke are coming from the roof which snaps me out of my daze.

"Let's move!" I shout as I take off toward the back of the building. No one aside from Vlad's guys know about that entry. I hear Andreas shouting orders to his men behind me but keep going, my brothers following my lead and are hot on my heels. As we round the corner two guys come into sight, before I can even draw my gun two shots ring out, each making a perfect hole in the center of the guys' forehead, each of them dropping to the ground. I owe Vin. I knew he was good but I didn't realize he was *that* good of a shot. My pace doesn't slow as I leap over one of their bodies, making my way to the door that is held open at the bottom by a brick. I attempt to go through but Bishop reaches and grips my elbow, pulling me back. The stench of smoke back here is strong.

"Don't be a hero," Bishop growls. "We go in but as a unit. Don't make any rash or stupid moves. Vincent can't cover us inside." I get what he is saying but right now I don't care about my safety. I care more about finding Anya.

"We need to split up. I'm not fucking leaving here without my brother!" Knight's tone brokers no room for argument. Right then Andreas and his guys find us.

Andreas darts his gaze between the four of us warily before speaking. "We going in or waiting to be shot?" Bishop shoots him a scathing look before turning his attention back to me.

"I always lead but, in this instance, I'm blind to the floor plan in there so lead us. Don't fuck up, Gage." I give a curt nod and don't stick around to trade more comments before I lead us all into the fray. Screams and shouts of help can be heard coming from the club side of the building. We rush down the red halls, half-naked girls are running from the rooms screaming and crying. Andreas barks orders to some of his guys to get these girls to safety and out of here. Shit turns sour when we round the corner, gunshots pop off. Our element of surprise is blown. Vlad's men are everywhere, my back is plastered flat against the wall. I turn to Bishop and find a look of outrage coated on his face. I look past him and that's when I see what has him so angry, Knight and King aren't with us, they have gone to find Rook.

"They'll be okay," I say, trying to appease him and keep his head in the game. He just grunts in response. When the shooting stops, Andreas uses hand signals to his men to fan out. I peek around the corner and that's when I see red. I draw my AK-47 to the front, flip it to full auto and let loose. The guards that are leading Vlad and Ivan from the office use their bodies as shields so those fuckers can get to safety. I don't stop, not even when the other fuckers start to shoot at me, I feel Bish and the others behind me shooting. I manage to drop a few of them with head shots. Bish and Andreas's guys take out the rest. For foot soldiers these guys are useless! They should have been able to take me out with a single shot, it shows what kind of a leader Vlad is when his own men can't even protect him.

I spoke too soon, we have been pinned down in the back end of the club for about ten minutes. We chased after Vlad and Ivan only to run straight into a fucking ambush. They were waiting for us in the club, right in the middle of the dance floor. Brock, Andreas, Bishop and I are holed up behind the DJ booth with a few other people that weren't able to get out before the shooting happened. The look of utter terror on their faces angers me, these are his fucking people and yet he doesn't try to barter or get them to safety. I know there is always casualties in a war but the loss of innocent lives is a toll that weighs heavy on me. If I can save a life, I will.

"We need to conserve our ammo, those fuckers aren't slowing and my COMS are down, I can't reach my guys." Andreas has lost a lot of his men tonight, I can see the devastation in his eyes. I still haven't seen Anya. I thought we could take those two fuckers down and then search for her. The fire is spreading and my guess is these fuckers are trying to keep us in here so we burn down with the club. "We need to find a way out, soon!" Andreas grits out.

"We should have waited for Tony." Bishop breaths out, a whoosh of air escapes me at his quietly spoken words. We thought by having a few more men than they do we could win this—truth is, we were fucking fools. We have come into their home thinking we knew the layout better. My need to get to Anya may have just cost us all our lives. The gunfire stops suddenly, Bish and I share a look loaded with unease.

"How long will you hide like the filthy fucking rats that you are?" Bishop's eyes darken, he grows ridged and clenches his gun at the sound of Mav's voice. I peer through the small gap between the stand and the stage that we are hiding behind, more than twenty guys stand there with guns aimed in our direction. Mav, the coward, stands in the middle with men all around him. I knew he was always a fucking pussy! "Come out Bishop and we'll let your little band of misfits go free." I shoot my brother a warning look, there is no fucking way he is going out there to that little bitch. Mav is a fucking rat and cannot be trusted. "You have thirty seconds to decide, if you don't, well... you know what will happen."

"I'm going out there–"

I cut Bishop off, not wanting to hear this shit. "Not going to fucking happen!" I seethe. "If you get killed, Kiara is going to chop my fucking balls off and I am quiet fucking fond of my nuts!" He grips the scruff of my shirt and hauls me close until we are nose to nose.

"Don't ever and I mean *ever*, let me hear you say anything about my fiancée and touching your dick again!"

"I said balls, not dick," I counter earning a growl from him and being shoved back into the stage.

"He will kill you the moment you step out there, I have no signal in here. They must have the place jammed up. I can't call for backup and your backup is still hours away." Bishop tries to hide his worry but fails. Andreas is right, we're fucked and we all know it. Someone is going to die in order for the rest of us to make it out of here. I refuse to let that someone be Bishop.

I tune back into Andrea's and Bishop's conversation. "...As soon as I have their attention, you lot run...." I tune them back out again when Mav begins to count backward from ten. I shoot my brother one last look. He's too focused on speaking with Andreas and the others to notice as I lay my rifle down and back away. I will not let any of my brothers pay the price for my stupidity. I should have made them wait but I was too eager to get to my girl. Unlike them, I don't have someone waiting on me back home... shit, I don't even think Anya would care if I lived or died honestly. I peer around the edge of the stage and fight the cough that threatens to break free, the smoke is getting thicker, I can feel the temperature rising as the fire draws nearer, moving from the back. Just as Mav gets to five, I step out with my hands raised, all eyes and guns turn to me.

"I'm here!" I call out.

"Gage, you fucking idiot!" I hear Bishop yell from behind me but I don't stop moving. I know Andreas and the others will be fighting to hold Bishop back. I keep my eyes on Mav, who is grinning like he won the fucking jackpot, as I call back to Bish.

"Tell the girls I love them, tell Car I'm sorry I won't be there to watch her marry Vin and tell King and Knight, I'm sorry I couldn't save Rook." When I stop in the middle of the dance floor, I take a deep breath before I utter the last words. "You were always my idol, Bishop. I never missed Tony or longed for a father figure because I always had you to look up to."

"Awwww, isn't that sweet. He finally admits he's a bitch out loud for the world to hear." I grit my teeth trying to tamper my anger and not allow Mav's word to set me off. "Truthfully, I would have loved to kill the Don but..." he steps out from behind the cover of his men and closes the space between us until he is a couple feet away. I notice that he favors his left side from when Vin shot him, but I also notice the blood soaking through his shirt near his abdomen. He follows my line of sight and smirks. "Oh, yeah, your bitch shot me." Pride swells inside me.

"Pity it wasn't a head shot," I snarl, his eyes darken as he strikes out and hits me across the jaw. I stumble back a step but right myself quickly and get ready to land a blow of my own until I hear all the guns cocking. Mav throws his head back and laughs like a fucking nut job, I need to do something so Bishop and the others can get out of here. I can hear the crackle of the fire, it won't be long before it breaches the back wall and Bishop and the others will be cornered.

"I got the bitch back, she won't be causing any more problems." All the blood drains from my face, my entire body feels like it's being weighed down by a ton of bricks. I search his gaze trying to detect if he is lying. I see it so clearly, he's telling the truth. Rage consumes me, I prepare myself for the onslaught of bullets that I know will come the moment I make a move but gunshots ring out from either side of the hall. I tackle Mav to the ground, I don't know who is fucking taking out the Bratva and right now I don't fucking care, all I want is to kill the son of bitch that took the life of the only woman that has made me feel something other than second best. He tries to push me off but it's futile, he's lost too much blood. I straddle him, gripping his face between my hands and stabbing my thumbs into his eyes. I push as hard as I can while smashing his head continuously into the wooden floor.

Chapter Twenty-Seven

Anya

I groan in pain and clutch my side. I wince from it, but I don't have the luxury of laying here and wallowing in self-pity that my cousin just fucking shot me.

"Alek!" I hear Ivan shout. I attempt to sit up but cry out in pain. I spy movement from my side and lift my gun, Krill smacks it out of the way as he yanks me to my feet, ignoring my cries of pain. He doesn't utter a word as he drags me to the door, unlocks it and yanks it open. He hides us behind the door while men pile in the room, fear grips me in its clutches.

We're going to die.

The thought is on repeat inside my head as Krill drags me out of the hiding spot. Ivan points to us and begins to curse me out in Russian, while eight guns are trained on us.

I eye each of them in confusion when they begin to trade looks amongst themselves, each of them looks worried. It baffles me why they would be scared of us when they could take the both of us out.

"Shoot and I pull the pin." I look up at Krill, confused as hell until I see the grenade in his hand. My eyes widen in surprise.

"Ty budesh' medlenno umirat' za eto," (*You'll die slowly for this*) Vlad promises as he climbs to his feet holding his *tiny* flesh wound like it's a gaping hole in his chest. Krill slowly backs us out of the room, never once daring to look behind us. I decide to be the eyes in the back of his head and peer over my shoulder. The hall has men with their guns aimed and at the ready. We take one step into the hall. I can tell they all have itchy trigger fingers and are ready to shoot.

"Propusti yeye!" (*Let her through*) I look between the four guys at the front to see Sasha standing there. He's one of the younger captains and I'll admit he was one of the hardest to turn. Sasha is loyal to a fault. He has no family and came up through the ranks quickly. Sasha isn't like the rest of the men here, he doesn't enjoy hurting and raping woman. The night I met with him to try and turn him, I had just came from a cage fight Vlad had set up because I was late on invoices. All it took was one look at how bruised I was and telling him Vlad set the fight as punishment for him to agree. I give him a curt nod and yank on Krill's shirt getting him to move faster. Thanks to the adrenaline pumping through my body, I can't feel the pain in my side but what I do feel, is the blood soaking my shirt.

Sasha motions for his men to let us through and they do. The guys from Vlad's office follow us out with their guns still raised but not willing to shoot Krill and risk blowing themselves up. Sasha and his men close the gap as soon as we are through, the right guys don't stand a chance. They are Vlad's puppets so Sasha orders his men to put them down. Krill drags me away and tries to lead us to the nearest exit but I pull free of his hold.

"I'm not leaving!" I say. He grits his teeth in agitation.

"You're shot and we are sitting fucking ducks, we need to go now!" I shake my head.

"You go. I'm going to burn this place to the fucking ground and kill those sons of bitches before I leave." I turn on my heel and head for my office where I have a stash of guns. Krill curses behind me, but follows after me nonetheless. If I don't end this now, there will be nowhere I will ever be able to hide where Vlad can't find me. I know my father, he may have tried to keep tabs on Koby and taken his time finding her but with me, I would be his sole focus and he would dedicate all his resources to finding me.

Once we reach my closet-size office, I rush to the filing cabinet and grab the first aid kit off the top. I make quick work of taping some gauze to my wound and fight back the tears that threaten to spill. This will have to do until I can get to a doctor, *if* I make it out of here alive. Krill tells me to get the guns while he creates a distraction. I finish dressing my wound and grab the guns from each of the places I hid them. They are only handguns but I have ammo as well. My office isn't big enough to have hidden rifles. I'm crouched behind my desk when the sound of a scream rings up. I peer over the top of my desk as I hear another and then Krill is charging.

"Move now, we have to do this fast before we're burnt alive!" I'm on my feet and handing him guns and loading my own as I ask him what he did. "Set a fire in the back to draw everyone to the front of the club, we need to get out of here and wait for them to come out the front."

"What if they don't?" I ask, feeling on edge about this plan of his. He smashes the magazine of his Glock into place before cocking the trigger back and meeting my stare.

"I blocked the back exits, ran into Sasha. He is going to guide them out the front and we'll be there waiting for him!" I'm about to protest when more screams sound out and the smell of smoke infiltrates my nose. "Let's move!"

Krill and I try to get as many girls as we can out of the building on our way out, some of them are so high they can barely walk. We haven't had to shoot a single person either. The captain's must have put out the word about changing sides, how they knew what was happening here tonight is unbeknown to me. If I had to guess, I would say Sasha put out the call letting them know. Krill is carrying a young girl that can't be any older than nine or ten, the track marks on her arms make me sick to my stomach. We break through into the club and it is utter chaos. Patrons are screeching and fighting to get out before the place burns down.

"We need to double back." I can hear the slight tremble of fear in his voice.

"No, you said we can take them out if we wait out front. I won't fucking lose this chance!" He turns to peer down at me, his face is a mask of irritation.

"We can't get out this way Anya–" Krill clamps his mouth closed and uses his body to push me against the wall with the young girl trapped between us. When the sound of gunshots erupt inside the club, I'm powerless to move him, not that I've tried because I'm loathed to admit it but I'm scared. Earlier I latched onto my anger and adrenaline to get me through. Now that is slowly draining from me, I'm beginning to feel the pain in my side. "Stay quiet, stay low and don't make a sound," Krill whispers close to my ear. I nod. "I can't move without risking them spotting me, can you see over my shoulder who it is?"

I do as he asks and peer around him the best that I can. I can't see who the group of people are running behind the stage thanks to the lighting their faces are cast in a shadow. But when I see the last guy drop to his knees and slide across the floor while firing off shots of his own, my breath hitches.

Gage.

He's here but, why?

I focus on the other group who are firing off round after not caring that some of their stray bullets are hitting innocent people, my chest constricts when I watch a man throw himself on top of a woman–who I assume is his girlfriend or wife. Two bullets hit him in the back, tears brim my eyes. He used his own body as a human shield to protect the one he loves.

Gage is pinned behind the stage, there is no exit back there. I saw at least eight of them dash behind the stage, they are outnumbered and clearly outgunned. I have to do something. I pull back and stare up at Krill, whatever he sees in my gaze has him tensing before letting out a long exhale. He and I both know how this night is going to play out, it's kill or be killed and I personally am okay with the latter.

"It's your American, isn't it?"

"Yeah, he's here but not alone," I whisper back.

"I can hear the shots, I don't need to see to know they are outmanned. We can't help him, Anya."

"No, we can't," Krill has been around me long enough to know that I agreed way too fast.

"But you have a plan?" I smile triumphantly.

"Yes, I do. The thing is, I'm too weak to do what needs to be done so I need your help."

"What do you need?" Relief flows through me at his agreement.

"Leave her with me, I need you to go find Sasha and tell him to get the other captain's out here. Tell him that this is the way they prove they are loyal to me by helping take down the men who are loyal to my father." Krill nods then slowly bends to place the girl on the ground at my feet. He quietly slips away, back the way we came. I pray to whoever may be listening that Krill makes it back in time with back up.

I stand here for what feels like hours waiting with bated breath for Krill return. The fire is closing in, it's so close I can hear it. Bodies of innocent patrons litter the floor, blood is everywhere. When the shooting stops, my ears ring from the sudden silence, my pulse wracks up a notch when I hear Alek speak, calling for Gage's brother. A part of me is glad he didn't call for Gage but another part hurts for him because he will have to watch his brother die.

"I'm here!" Gage calls out and my blood turns to ice as he walks out from the behind the stage with his hands in the air.

"Gage, you fucking idiot!" Bishop screams out, the agony in his tone is clear.

"Tell the girls I love them, tell Car I'm sorry I won't be there to watch her marry Vin and tell King and Knight, I'm sorry I couldn't save Rook." He pauses for a beat before taking a deep breath and continuing. "You were always my idol, Bishop. I never missed Tony or longed for a father figure because I always had you to look up to."

"Awwww, isn't that sweet. He finally admits he's a bitch out loud for the world to hear." Alek sounds like a smug son of a bitch. "Truthfully, I would have loved to kill the Don but..." It gives me great joy to watch him limp and know he is in pain because of me. "Oh, yeah, your bitch shot me."

"Pity it wasn't a head shot." I smile at the proudness I hear in Gage's voice. I grit my teeth and clench my fists at my sides when Alek hits Gage.

"I got the bitch back, she won't be causing any more problems." Everything happens so fast, Gage and Alek are on the floor, gunfire from either side of the room. Bishop and the others rushing out from behind the stage, it is utter carnage.

Chapter Twenty-Eight

Gage

Pop.

I feel the moment my thumbs pierce his eye balls but I don't stop smacking his head against the floor. He's motionless beneath me–dead. But I can't stop. This piece of shit tried to have my sister killed, and gave up Kiara's location in New England so her father could find her. He got Ally kidnapped and snitched to our enemies that Knight was fighting at the shack. If Koby didn't turn up when she did, my brother would be dead. He shot *my* girl! He fucking took her from me! I can hear my name being called but I can't discern who it is because of my pulse roaring in my ears.

I feel a hand land on my forearm, I snap my gaze to the person and freeze. "Stop. He's dead." I tear my thumbs from his eyes and reach for her, cupping her face with my bloody hands. She smiles tentatively at me but I need to *feel* her. I yank her to me and smash my lips against hers, she opens for me instantly like I knew she would. I try to deepen the kiss but she backs off and hisses, I follow her line of sight to her side and gently lift her shirt to see blood soaking through a bandage.

"Let's move!" Bishop shouts. I look around to see Mav's guys lying dead on the floor in a pool of their own blood. I hop to my feet and gently help Anya's to hers. I try to drag her behind me but she pulls free of my hold.

"We need to go. This place is going to burn down and we'll be trapped if we don't leave now," I say in a rush but she shakes her head.

"I know where he is and I won't leave until this is finished. I have to do this, Gage." I growl in frustration before cupping her face between my hands and staring down into her eyes that hold so much pain and anger.

"I'll help you but we need to get out of here–." The back wall bursts into flames, shouts sound out around the room as everyone rushes for the exit. Not wanting to argue further, I pick her up bride style and cringe when she cries out in pain. "I'm sorry," I say as I run for the exit. I spot Bishop in the distance scanning the room, when his gaze lands on me I see him visibly relax. He waits for us and ushers me ahead of him. We break out into the nighttime air and I breathe a relieved sigh for the first time all night. I don't stop moving until we are across the street. I turn us back and watch as the building goes up in flames. The heat of the fire can be felt from over here. It brings me great pleasure to watch as that fucking torture palace burns to the ground.

"I need to find the others." Bishop's words pull me back

to the present. Shit, I forgot Knight and King took off to find Rook. Just as I'm about to reply to Bishop, I spot King running toward us from the other end of the street. He looks like shit and has blood covering him. but he doesn't look injured so the blood isn't his. Bishop pulls him into a hug when reaches us. King pulls back and looks from me to the girl in my arms and smiles.

"Welcome to the family," he says to Anya, who just frowns as I smirk at my brother. He may know, but Anya has no idea that me coming for her tonight means she is mine for keeps. "Bish, we need to go after the twins, now!" The urgency in King's tone tells me something fucking bad has happened. Bishop gets right in his face and growls out,

"Where the fuck are they?" Before King has a chance to answer, Vincent fucking appears out of nowhere and scares the fucking shit out of me! I shoot him a fucking glare that he ignores as he focuses on Bishop.

"They followed Ivan and Vlad, stole someone's car and chased after them. I couldn't get a clear shot so I took out their wheels, they wouldn't have gotten far." Bishop and King both take off toward the SUV's that we pulled up in and climb in. Vin isn't far behind them. I'm torn on going after my brothers and helping Anya.

"Either carry me to the car or put me the fuck down. I'm going with or without you!" I stare at her wide eyed for a second until a horn honks, pulling me from my stupor. I take off toward the others and climb in while gently placing her in the middle of me and Vin. Bish doesn't wait for me to close the door before he is burning rubber. Vin calls out directions. I have no fucking idea how Vincent knows where they went but I do remember Car saying he is the best tracker.

"Your brother is... he needs help." I peer down at Anya

confused. Bishop and King are fine I think to myself. "Rook, Gage, I'm talking about Rook."

"What the hell is that supposed to mean?" comes from King. She darts her tongue out to moisten her lips and twiddles with the end of her shirt not meeting his gaze.

"H-he was there when Ivan... when he..." A string of curses come from me. Vincent is gritting his teeth in rage. King's eyes are burning with vengeance and Bishop is white knuckling the steering wheel. We all knew it was a possibility that she could have been... raped, but hearing it from her and knowing it was her uncle has me seeing red.

"He won't make it out of the country, you have my word. Your father and uncle will both die tonight." Bishop's promise hangs in the air. I can tell he means it and if Bishop promises something you can guarantee he will always deliver.

"Left here!" Vin calls out. Bishop maneuvers the car down a side street and we can see taillights ahead. Bishop puts his foot flat to the floor as he races to catch up. We follow behind the small blue sedan, the street is one way with cars parked either side so we can't get in front of the twins. We know it's them, plus the driver giving us the bird out the window and then waving, definitely gave the dumbasses away. I can see sparks flying off the SUV in front of the twins, they are down to the rims now and won't make it much further.

"Vlad is mine," Anya announces to the car. No one in here disagrees, truthfully all we want is for them both to be dead. "Ivan, he needs to be kept alive." That has me, Vin and King staring at her and Bish eyeing her in the rearview mirror.

"Why the fuck would you want him alive?" I snarl.

Vincent cocks his head to the side and studies her for a second before he speaks.

"You don't want him alive for *you*, you want him alive for another reason and someone else." It's not a question, it's a statement.

"Yes," she whispers.

"For who?" King demands. She slowly lifts her gaze to me as she answers King.

"Rook." Sharp intakes of air can be heard throughout the car. "You didn't see what I saw. He needs to be the one to do it or your brother will not come back to you. He has already lost himself, you can see it in his eyes, Gage. He will need to be the one to do it but he cannot do that tonight, he is still too frightened of Ivan." Before any of us can answer, Bishop jams on the breaks and leaps from the car, Vin and King follow. I jump out and hold up a hand to Anya who glares at me. "I'm coming!" I grit my teeth and help her from the car, the stubborn set of her jaw and the promise of pain in her gaze told me she would just follow even if I said no. Two gunshots ring out and on instinct I push Anya behind me. Cries of pain can be heard coming from the front of the SUV that carried her father and uncle.

"Move again and I'll blow out your kneecap!" Bishop's tone is ice cold and filled with hatred. We pass the car the twins were in and I peek inside to see Rook sitting in the passenger seat with his head down. I grip Anya's hand and pull her behind me as we reach my brothers and Vin. Vlad is on the ground clutching his knee, a man who I assume was their driver lays on his back with a hole in the middle of his head. Ivan is on his knees with his hands in the air, Knight stands behind him with a fistful of his hair in his grip and a knife to his throat.

"You are going to pay for this—" Vlad clamps his mouth

closed when Anya pulls free of my grip and moves into his sight. He stares at her with disgust. How a man can father a child and hate them is something I will never understand. "You betrayed your own family, you ungrateful bitch! I should have killed you when I had the chance." Bishop lifts his gun ready to end Vlad but Anya reaches out and places her hand on his arm, stopping him. They share a look for a few seconds before Bish hands her his gun. She takes a step forward and winces but tries her best to hide her pain. I notice that she is pale and unsteady on her feet. She needs to see a fucking doctor!

"All my life, all I ever wanted was for you to be proud of me, to love me, look at me the way you looked at Alek. I was nothing but an object for you to use whenever you felt like it. I make one mistake and I'd have to fight for my life." Hearing her say this out loud has my heart breaking for her. Anya Volkov is one strong fucking woman and I'm proud to say she is *my* woman.

Chapter Twenty-Nine

Anya

I used to fear my father but now as I stand here and stare down at the pathetic excuse for a man, I feel stupid. He is nothing more than a glorified thug. He hid behind his men and made his wealth on the pain of others.

"You will die here tonight on this dark deserted road, alone and unloved. But, before you die I want you to know something. First, your men are now loyal to me and *I* am the Pakhan to the Volkov Bratva and will lead them in a new direction that doesn't involve using women or stealing children from their beds so I can line my pockets." Satisfaction rolls through me as his face morphs into a shocked look. "Second, I have known where Katarina is this whole time." I can feel Knight's gaze on me but I don't stop. "Dante and I helped her and Dimitri flee Russia to get away from you."

His upper lip pulls back in a snarl. "Katarina is pregnant, she is happy and in love." His eyes widen as I smirk and turn to look at Knight who stares at Vlad with a smile so wide it almost looks unreal. "Third, your precious Alek is dead." Both Vlad and Ivan start mouthing off but I push on. "It was the greatest sight I have ever seen to watch as Gage bashed his skull in and pushed his thumbs through that bastards eye sockets."

Vlad mouths off again. "You will never rule, my men will never follow a whore much less one that is spreading her legs like a drive through for a fucking American *suka*."

"He may be a lot of things but a *bitch* isn't one of them. Lastly, I want you to die knowing that you never broke me. Your brother may have raped me and brutalized my body, but he never broke me, you robbed me of my right to bear children and still, I stand here unbroken. I hope you burn in hell for all of eternity." I don't wait for him to respond, I lift the gun and pull the trigger. I shoot him in the head once, twice in the chest and twice in the dick for good measure before I turn to Ivan. His eyes widen, gone is the sure of himself cocky look that he always wears. His eyes are wide and his face pale, the prick is shaking like a leaf. I move toward him but sway slightly, within a second Gage is beside me holding me upright.

"You need to see a doctor," he says low enough for only me to hear. I smile up at him and nod.

"I will, I just need to do this." He nods stiffly as I turn back to Ivan. "You thought you were untouchable because of who your brother is–sorry, *was*. I'm here to tell you that you are not. You will not meet a swift end like Vlad, your death will be drawn out. You won't see it coming, or know when it is coming until it is too late. You will suffer for the things you have done, for the lives you have ruined. It disgusts me that I share blood with you. I want you to hear me loud and clear. I am the last living Volkov and that name will die with me, not you, not your brother and certainly not your good for nothing son." His eyes blaze anger, he tries to move which causes Knight to dig the blade into his throat cutting it slightly. "I hope Rook destroys you—mind body and soul." His brows furrow in confusion, making me release a humorless laugh. "Oh, dear uncle, I am not going to kill you, after all you are not mine to kill." I don't wait for his reply as I turn and walk away. A sense of relief washes over me, feeling like the weight of the world has been lifted from my shoulders now that two of the three are dead. Ivan will die soon enough, but knowing his death will be dragged out gives me great satisfaction.

With no destination in sight and not wanting to drive around all night, I told Gage to take us to Vlad's house–my house. Bishop and Knight chose to stay back and deal with Ivan, *keeping him out of sight* as they put it. I didn't care to learn what that meant. Rook, King, Gage, Vin and I all ride silently together. Gage and I sit in the middle seats with Rook. He hasn't uttered a single word, he won't look anyone in the eye or even return a hug. He is safe now and out of danger but for some reason he seems more withdrawn now than when I last saw him with Ivan.

I've been feeling dizzy for the last twenty minutes and know it's because I am still losing blood. I managed to contact Krill with a phone we found in the console. He and Vor promised to meet me at the house with a doctor. Gage wraps his arm around my shoulders and draws me into his side. I rest my head against him and sigh.

"What's your next move, killer?" he asks quietly. I ponder for a few moments and for the first time in years I don't have a plan.

"I don't know exactly. I guess clean up the mess Vlad made and try to rebuild from there," I answer honestly.

"So, you're gonna stay in Russia?" The hurt in his tone guts me, I don't want to hurt him but the truth is, I have no idea what we even are to each other. Do I care about him? Yes. Do I love him? I didn't think I did until tonight. People say you learn to love over time and it doesn't happen instantly, but for me I don't need time. From the moment I saw his picture and watched him from afar for weeks, I grew fascinated by him. Then I met him, spent time with him and something inside me changed. Gage gave me hope. For so many years I had none and was resigned to the fact I would die by my father's order.

"Gage..." I cut myself off when we pull into the driveway and I spot Krill and a few others leaning against a sleek black car. Gage pulls away from me and it hurts but I get it, we need to talk but now isn't the time for that.

After the doctor stitches me up and dresses my wound, he left me some amazing pain pills that I have to take daily. I managed to shower and change into some of my own clothes I left here. I flinch in pain as I slip under the covers of my bed. I'm just about to turn the lights out when a knock sounds at the door. I call out to whoever it is to come in and I'm shocked when I see it's Andreas.

"Can I come in?" I pull myself into a sitting position and grit my teeth through the pain. Once seated, I motion for him to enter. He stands at the foot of my bed with his hands in his pockets, a weird look on his face. Tension and awkwardness are thick in the air. Not so long ago we were enemies and now... now I have no idea what we are. "If you had of asked me twelve hours ago if I could ever see myself inside Vladimir's Volkov's house, I would have laughed in your face." We both laugh and it helps to break some of the awkwardness.

"What are you doing here, Andreas?" He pushes his mouth to the side and shoots me a look of gratitude.

"You saved my life, Anya."

"No–"

"Don't be coy, you did and you and I both know it. You could have killed me but you didn't, why?" Well that feels like a loaded question!

"Call me crazy, but I had hoped by me not killing you, a moment like this would play out in the future. Of course, in my vision I was on my feet and not lying in bed with a bullet wound."

"What happens now?" I slump back against the headboard.

"Now, I try to fix what he broke but I'm going to need your help. I-I have a choice to make and I'm going to choose what I want." He furrows his brow in confusion but that's okay. I know what I want and I'm going to get it, I just need to fix shit here first. Andreas and I sit here and make a plan for the future. Everything seemed so grim an hour ago but now I feel like we can make this work. After an hour or so, Andreas bids me goodnight and leaves. I wait for a long time, hoping Gage will come find me but after another hour, I decide he isn't coming and turn the lights out to get some rest, tomorrow is going to be a long-ass day.

I'm roused from my slumber by the feeling of soft lips

kissing a trail from my mouth to my ear. "I love you." I keep my eyes closed but can't fight the smile from breaking free. The last time I heard those three little words was the day Katarina left. His arms slip around me gently so he doesn't hurt me, gently shifts in closer and rests his chin on my shoulder. "I can't leave you behind. I was never supposed to fall for you, killer. I was sent here to take down your family, that was my only task. Instead, I met you and suddenly things weren't just black and white anymore. I can't leave Russia without you. If I could stay I would but I have to... my family needs me." I place my hand atop of his and give it a gentle squeeze.

"Then don't leave without me," I whisper.

"I can't stay." The heartache in his voice devastates me. I roll over so we are facing each other and reach up to cup his face.

"I know, give me three months max and I'll board that plane with you." His brows raise in surprise.

"But what about the Bratva?" I smile lovingly back at him and place a peck to his lips.

"I love you, Gage Murdoch. For the first time I am choosing me over my sense of duty to my people. Andreas is going to take over the Bratva and run things here while I move to the US, with you." He doesn't say anything for a while and I start to think I have gotten the wrong idea about him wanting me to move. "If this isn't what you—" He silences me with a kiss that steals my breath, pouring everything he feels for me into this kiss, and it has me seeing stars. When he pulls back we're both panting and trying to pull in lungfuls of air.

"I love that you called me a Murdoch." I smile and kiss him again. "I'll help you however I can. I'll also be here for you to talk to about what you went through. I know shit is going to be hard but I need you to know I'm in this for the long haul, killer."

Gage held me while I talked, I'm not even close to ready to even entertain the idea of sex. I told him about what happened to me. He held me tighter, promising me that no matter what, he still loved me and wouldn't look at me differently. I believe him. He even offered to have a shrink that one of his brothers hired for his fiancée come speak with me about what happened when we land in the States. I agreed, I think it would be good for me to speak to someone about the trauma I have experienced throughout my life.

Chapter Thirty

Gage

Eight weeks later...

It's been nearly four months since we first arrived here in Russia, we fly out tomorrow and I couldn't be happier. Bish and the others have gone for haircuts and even decided to fucking shave so they look their best for the girls. Knight is the most excited and anxious, he wants to get home so he can be there for Koby when she goes into labor. Shit, I just found out last night that both Car and Kiara are pregnant as well. I'm beyond happy for all of them, they deserve this. Anya has been making huge progress. She hasn't let what happened to her define or change her. Her famous words as of late are *I'm not a victim, I'm a survivor.* She is fucking strong. She had bad night terrors for the first month but they have started to lessen over the weeks. Her wound has almost healed completely and she is able to get around much better now. She wanted to shut me out and deal with it on her own, but I wasn't having that. I forced my way through her walls and molded myself deep inside her. She knows she is everything to me and I would burn the fucking world to the ground if it meant she would be happy.

I have barely left her side for more than five minutes in the past weeks. She assures me she is fine but until Bishop gives up the location of her fucking uncle, I can't handle having her out of my sight. She has been working closely with Andreas and Bishop to hand over the Bratva. Bish is here negotiating terms with the new Pakhan on how they will move forward. Andreas has made it clear there will be no trafficking of any kind, women and children will be protected from now on. Bishop has agreed to trial using Andreas as a supplier for guns. The one thing Anya has refused to give up is her formula for shipping drugs.

"I'll give you everything you need and never try to claim it back," she says to Andreas. Bishop and Andreas occupy the seats in front of her desk at her house—Vlad's old one. King and Vin lean against the back wall with their arms crossed over their chests. We haven't seen much of Knight, he spends every day with his twin trying to coax him to talk or even come out of his room, but he refuses. Because of who our family is, we cannot show weakness. Once we are in the privacy of our own home, then we can deal with Rook and try to help him heal from the ordeal he went through. He was a prisoner for nearly eight months. He has scars on the surface and internally, that will take way longer than eight weeks to heal.

"But?" Andreas pushes.

"I will not give up my formula for shipping narcotics.

Either of you want to ship internationally then you do it through me. This is the one thing my father could never take away from me and I won't let either of you take it from me either." I place both my hands on the tops of her shoulders and give them a squeeze, telling her silently that I'm proud of her for standing her ground.

"If what I have heard is true, then I look forward to doing business with you," Bishop says then cuts his gaze to me. "Be warned, just because you are with my brother does not mean I will tolerate tardiness or you fucking me over." He pulls his gaze from me to stare at my girl. I want to butt in and tell him to fuck off, but this is business and not my place. "Business will not be mixed with personal things. Now I must warn you of something." I feel her tense and fight the smile that wants to break free, I know what he is going to say next. "My fiancée, sister and Ally won't welcome you with open arms like Koby will."

"Why?" Anya queries.

"Because you are dating their... best friend." I know that pained him to admit and fuck it makes me feel warm inside knowing my relationship with Kiara still bothers him. "They are protective over him. Prove to them you mean him no harm and that your feelings are true, and you should have no problems."

"And if there are problems, how should I handle that?" Bishop shakes his head laughing. King and Vin push off the wall and move forward both wearing smiles.

"If Kiara and Gucci weren't pregnant, they would drive you to the gym and fight it out in the ring." Vin sounds so proud that his girl can throw down. Anya's brows jump up, a slow smirk graces her beautiful face as she turns to King waiting to hear what he has to say.

"Look, I love my girl and cherish her but when Ally gets

angry, I tend to step back and allow her to take the lead or I risk becoming dickless, and I'm not down with that." Everyone begins to laugh. Everyone thinks because we are *the* mafia that us guys run the show. Truth is, the girls have us all by the balls and there is nothing we wouldn't do for them. "Look, Ally isn't the one you need to watch out for. Kiara is crazy loyal to Gage and will give you a hard time. Car loves Gage and only wants what is best for her brother. Just be grateful Koby is your friend because that woman would be the worst to deal with. Ally has always been closest to the twins, her attention will be... elsewhere." King doesn't need to say more, we all know what he is saying without using the words.

By the time we fall into bed we are both tired and spent from the long-ass day of tying up loose ends and packing. She has decided to keep her house and a few others around the world that Vlad owned, saying we might want to travel and check them out some day. Who am I to argue with her? She told me today she would have to come back every couple months to check production of her *business* as we are calling it. To my complete and utter shock, she went to Vor and Krill and asked them if they would work for her and oversee her business while she was away. Needless to say they both agreed and were happy as fuck with their new positions and pay raise.

"I'm sorry." I roll over and stare at her confused, she lulls her head side and smiles. Seeing her eyes fill with tears has me panicking.

"What's going on, killer?" She reaches out and grips my

hand in hers as the first tear falls. Anya doesn't cry so seeing her cry now has me worrying.

"I wish more than anything I would be able to see a miniature version of me and you running around but I can never give you that, Gage." I open my mouth to argue but she shushes me and pushes on. "I can never give you children and if that is a deal breaker for you, then I... I understand." She sobs, I growl as I maneuver myself until I am on top of her. She doesn't freeze now whenever I climb on top, she is slowly exploring my body nightly until she grows more comfortable. I'll never push her.

"Get that shit out your fucking head now. Don't you dare sit there and act like you're not it for me, Anya. You are more than I could ever ask for." Tears flow freely down her cheeks. I lean down and kiss them away, hating that she feels like this. I know it bothers her and she tries to push me away more often than not because she thinks I will grow to resent her for not being able to have kids, but I have been doing research of my own. "Did you know that you still ovulate even after having a hysterectomy?" She frowns up at me and shakes her head. "You don't get your period but you still produce eggs. If we wanted to, we could explore that option and look into a surrogate if it's something that we wanted to do in the future." She wraps her arms around my neck and pulls me down so she can kiss me. After a couple seconds, I pull back and roll off her, shooting her a sheepish smile.

"What happened?"

"Killer, you're a blonde bombshell with a fucking killer body and the most delectable tits known to mankind."

"I'm not following?"

"Baby, my cock is rock hard so I need a cold shower... again." She throws her head back and laughs as I head for the adjoining bathroom. Just as I pass through the threshold, she calls out to me, I peer over my shoulder and quirk a brow.

"I love you, Gage Murdoch." My heart soars inside my chest hearing those words from her.

"I love you too, Anya-soon-to-be-Murdoch." Her eyes widen to the size of saucers. I leave her to stew on that while handle *my* business in the shower.

Rook

I should have felt free being on the plane heading back to New York. I didn't.

I should have felt happiness when we pulled into the driveway and seen the girls standing there waiting for us with open arms. I didn't.

I should feel some sense of nostalgia or belonging standing in the middle of my old room. I don't feel anything.

I look around the photos that litter the tops of my dressers, my walls, my desk but the person I see in those isn't me—not anymore. His brown eyes hold laughter, freedom, love—mine hold none. His brown hair is styled perfectly with not a hair out of place—mine is long and messy. He looks like he spends hours a day at the gym and takes pride in himself and his appearance. I struggled to even shower and change before the flight, not caring what I look like. My door opens without a knock sounding, I don't even bother turning around because I know it's him.

"Hey, dude, we're gonna order in some takeout and hang out in the living room. You should come join us." It pains me to hear the longing in his voice but I can't appease him by plastering a fake smile on my face and acting like I didn't go through hell. I shake my head, I haven't spoken a word to anyone, I'm too scared. "Rook–"

"Do you mind if I try?" I tense at the sound of Anya's voice, out of everyone here she is the one who knew what was happening. She saw me at my lowest fucking point and what I did... willingly all because I was too much of a bitch to risk being punished again.

"Uh, yeah, okay. If you change your mind, brother, you know where to find us." I nod, still not bothering to turn around and acknowledge him. When I hear the door click, I stiffen further when I feel her draw near. She doesn't stop until she stands in front of me. I keep my gaze focused over her head, not wanting to look at her face and see the similarities to Ivan.

"I just want you to know, I have not uttered a word to anyone about what happened." That draws my attention. I stare down at her making sure to keep all emotion off my face. "What you went through..." I narrow my eyes in warning, she swallows and nods, understanding not to go there or risk me losing it. "Ivan is alive and he is yours to kill... when you are ready." This isn't news to me, Knight already told me. She releases a long exhale, nods curtly and heads for the door, but pauses. "I just thought you should know, I had all the girls released and sent home or to rehab. Andreas and I set up a shelter for them. We will never let what happened to them or... you happen to anyone else." She opens the door and the sound of Bishop's booming voice draws both our attention. I slowly follow her from the room, but instead of racing down the stairs like she does, I stay in the shadows and peer over the railing. Bishop and the others stand in a united line facing off against someone who I can't see.

"How the fuck did she get in here?" King asks.

"Luka!" Bishop calls for his right-hand man again, who comes rushing into the foyer looking panicked.

"Yes, boss?"

"Want to tell me how the fuck a skinny little girl made it past my security and got into my house?" Luka opens his mouth but no words come out, he moves in closer and his face pales.

"What the fuck are you doing here, Clare?" Everyone down there exchanges curious looks before staring at Luka waiting for an explanation.

"Come on, you didn't call or text for weeks and all you say is chasing down a missing brother." I grip the railing and grit my teeth in anger as she so carelessly says that. "I got worried, so I flew out here to see if you were alive and to get a peek at the missing brother." My brothers and the girls snicker, while Luka turns a bright shade of red.

"Fucking hell, Clare, get your shit. You'll be on the next plane back to OKC tonight." He grips her arm and starts to drag her toward the front door. I move out of the shadows trying to get a better look at her. As if she can sense me she looks straight up and her bright green eyes clash with mine. Her long brown hair is tied into a high ponytail. She is skinny and fragile looking, I can see faint bruises on her arms. Anger soars inside me seeing those marks on her skin. I take another step and knock a vase off its perch, drawing everyone's attention to me. Luka pauses. I don't pay any of them any attention as I focus on the girl who stares directly back at me. Recognition shines in her eyes, my eyes widen at the same time hers do.

"Rook?" she breathes my name and it fucking cracks something inside me hearing my name from her lips.

"How the fuck do you know him, Clare?" Luka demands, she just shakes her head and moves away from everyone heading up the stairs toward me without ever breaking eye contact. She stops a few feet away, running her gaze over me in a way that makes me think she is checking for injury. I scoff, Clare doesn't care about anyone but herself, I learned that the hard way.

"I didn't know it was you. I'm so sorry, Rook." When she reaches for me, I pull away and glare at her. Hurt clouds her features and it has my anger soaring to new heights. I haven't seen her in years and now, after all this time she shows up randomly at my house and somehow knows Luka.

"Don't ever touch me again." Gasps sound out from downstairs at hearing me speak for the first time in weeks. My voice is coarse and raspy from not being used for months, but it feels good to finally break my silence, even if it is to tell the girl who broke my world apart to fuck off. "You lost that right the night you ran from me and killed my kid."

Click the link to read Rook's story,
Ruined By The Rook

Wow, what a freaking ride, right?
I know you probably hate me for the cliffhanger... again.
Rest assured, Rook's book will be out very soon, be warned
his book will be the darkest in the whole series....
I'm so glad you all got to see a different side of Gage and
how amazing he truly is. I think out of everyone he deserved
his happy ending. Anya is no meek mouse either and that
girl went through some hard shit but she came out on top.
I have loved writing each of these books and always knew
from the start that Gage would have a book, there has
always been something about him that I've loved.
If you loved Gage and Anya's book, please leave a review on
Amazon, Bookbub or **Goodreads**, it would mean a
lot to hear your feedback.

Mafia Romance

<u>Murdoch Mafia Series</u>

Played By The Bishop

Tormented By The King

Tortured By The Knight

Tempted By The Queen

Turned By The Pawn

Ruined By The Rook

<u>Murdoch Mafia Novella</u>

Stalemate

<u>Memento Mori Series</u>

Reign Of Royal

Broken By Sin

In Havoc Lays Chaos

<u>Godfathers of the night</u>

London has Fallen

Damned By His Angel

<u>Re Della Strada</u>

Shattered Soul

Fractured Heart

Tainted Essence

<u>Fairytales With A Twist</u>

Condemned Beast

Secret Society/ Bully

Filthy Few

Forever Filthy

Filthiest Of Them All

Masked Men Novella (Pure Smut)

Dirty Priest

Dirty Daddy

Sports Romance

<u>Playing For Keeps</u>

Offside

Touchdown

End Game

Hail Mary

Blindside

RH Sports

Hate Us Like You Mean It

MM

Love Me Like You Mean It

Paranormal Romance

<u>The Veil Of Obsidian</u>

Of Time And Carnage

<u>Curse Of Fate</u>

Dream

Fate

Nightmare

Redemption

Anarchy

<u>Brutal Savages</u>

Savage Lies

Brutal Truth

Savage Beast

Brutal Beauty

ACKNOWLEDGMENTS

Firstly, my parents. I am who I am today because of the both of you and I love that neither of you ever tried to diminish my outrageous personality or tame my flare.

My man, my muse, my inspiration, Marcus. You inspire me to write all the torture scenes in this series because you piss me off. The make-up sex is fucking epic, so I'm not complaining!

Tash and Clare, thank you both for beta reading all of these books and supporting me throughout the whole process. You both are so freaking amazing for my ego, I appreciate you both so very much.

Thank you so freaking much to Jaye Pratt for formatting these books! The gorgeous headers are all thanks to Jaye!

My ARC and Street team, thank you ladies so freaking much for all the work that you do and always pushing me to give each of these guys the stories they deserve.

My babies, my rat bags, my world. I love you both so freaking much it hurts. You both inspire me daily to continue to chase my dreams and never give up. Chase your dreams, my loves, because the sky's the limit for you both.

My amazing editor Liz, thank you for all the work you do on each of these books. They are perfect because of the magic you weave, I'm so glad I found you!

My readers,

Thank you from the bottom of my heart for reading my

book. Without you none of this would be possible. I wouldn't be able to live out my dream if it wasn't for each of you so thank you, thank you, thank you.

Sam

ABOUT THE AUTHOR

Samantha Barrett is a dark romance, PNR author who loves to write out-of-the-box stories. She is originally from the land of the long white cloud, New Zealand. She is totally fluking her way through this whole author gig, if she isn't writing you can find her kicking back with her kids and husband with a bag of chips and a glass of wine in her hand. Sam loves Twilight and is a TWIHARD proudly.

www.ingramcontent.com/pod-product-compliance
Lightning Source LLC
Chambersburg PA
CBHW030025200726
48283CB00012B/1029